The Thrice Named Man

Part IV

Transsilvanian

The Thrice Named Man

Part IV

Transsilvanian

by

Hector Miller

www.HectorMillerBooks.com

The Thrice Named Man

Part IV

Transsilvanian

Author: Hector Miller

Proofreading: Kira Miller, J van Rensburg, Carly Weii

First edition, 2019, Hector Miller

Part IV in the book series The Thrice Named Man

ISBN: 9781090669711

Contents

Contents (continued)

Contents (continued)

Chapter 1 – Exile (October 244 AD)

Hostilius gazed across the wide water, made grey by the overcast sky. His eyes settled on the southern bank, more than a Roman mile distant.

He laughed a cold laugh, deprived of humour, and spat into the Danube. "To Hades with them", he said, and turned his back on the lands of Rome.

I sat on the rotting bole of a long fallen oak, beset by a dark mood, meticulously running a whetstone along the blade of my gladius.

Segelinde was asleep in the tent, covered with furs. Thirty paces downriver, Arité, now three, played with her doll close to the trees. The howl of a wolf split the silence, nearly causing me to topple from the log.

An apparition materialised from the mogshade five paces from the little girl, his elongated skull emphasized by swirling blue tattoos. In his right hand he carried a war axe, still covered with bright blood. A strung bow was slung over his shoulder.

The little girl screamed with joy, ran to Gordas and hugged his leg.

During our flight from the farm, following the murder of my father, Arité spent most of her time riding with either myself or

Gordas, as we were the best horsemen. Needless to say, even with the language barrier, they took to each other from the start, leaving me with pangs of jealousy every time my daughter ran to him.

From a leather satchel the Urugundi warrior produced a growling wolf cub.

"Uncle Gorra, you got one, you got one!" she yelled, and jumped up to reach it, her golden hair contrasting starkly against Gordas's dark aura.

He placed the snarling cub on the sand between them. "He is hungry, Princess", he said in Scythian.

The Hun champion produced a furry package of animal skin.

Aritê all but grabbed it from him and unwrapped it to reveal small chunks of bloody meat.

The wolf sniffed the air cautiously, but soon he was gorging on the meat. Afterwards he licked the blood off Aritê's hands, to her obvious delight.

"What is his name?" Marcus asked.

My daughter answered without hesitation. "His name is Nik because he loves me."

Nobody replied, as the wounds were still raw. I had to swallow back emerging emotions of loss, self-pity, anger and hatred.

"Primus Pilus, walk with me", I said, and gestured for Marcus and Cai to join us.

"So what's your plan, Domitius?" Hostilius asked when we were out of earshot.

"I don't have one", I replied.

I held up my hand to stop his retort. "But I have this."

I produced the small scrap of parchment given to me weeks earlier.

"When we were camped on the plain south of Carrhae, the legate of the Third Gallica gave me this. Just before we were exiled by the Arab."

I handed it to Marcus and he read out loud. *"You saved us all. We will not forget. You have friends."*

"The legate of the Third is Publius Licinius Valerianus", Marcus said. "He has a son, Gallienus, who is about my age. They descend from a well-respected senatorial family. Both are military men at heart."

Hostilius growled in reply. "Well-respected my arse. Most of these men, who sacrifice the lives of thousands of the common soldiers to line their own pockets, are 'well-respected'. I, for one, am done with Rome."

I looked at Marcus to solicit his view.

He sighed. "I would prefer to return, but alas, I do not think it is possible."

I turned to Cai for his opinion, but he returned my gaze with the blank stare of the easterners.

I could not return to my mother's people, the Roxolani. I had given an oath to Octar, the king of the Urugundi Huns, that I would not. Thiaper invited me to stay with the Carpiani. In the same manner, both Kniva and Rodoulphos offered us sanctuary with the Thervingi Goths and the Heruli.

Kniva, my brother-in-law, was well-liked by us all. Even Marcus and Hostilius had befriended the Gothic iudex.

"Then the choice is obvious, we will go to the Thervingi Goths", I said.

Hostilius asked the question we all wanted the answer to. "Will they expect us to fight by their side if they war with Rome?"

"Remember, Primus Pilus, Rome and the Goths renewed their peace when they signed the foedus agreement a year or two ago", I replied. "Rome pays them an annual tribute so there will be no fighting. Same goes for the Carpiani."

Kniva and the rest of our companions arrived back at the camp after their hunting excursion. My brother-in-law speared a huge boar and the Huns felled a young deer.

Soon we had a roaring fire going.

Aritê was sitting on Kniva's knee. "Tell me about the hunt again, Uncle Knee."

Kniva patiently repeated the happenings of the day and re-enacted the way he speared the boar. Little Nik was content, lying close by, his stomach filled with fresh meat.

Segelinde was the one to tell Kniva. "Brother, we have decided to take you up on your offer of hospitality. We will not be a burden to you as we have brought enough coin to pay our way."

Kniva smiled. "I was hoping that you would."

He drank from his cup and continued. "You are the sister of the king, Segelinde. For you to pay for anything would be a slap in my face. What is mine is yours."

We started to protest, but he waved it away.

It turned out to be a fine evening. I drank a bit too much wine and fell asleep the moment I lay down.

I rode Simsek across the Sea of Grass, the Danube at my back. In the distance, to my left, I saw the camp of the Roxolani and

5

pulled on the reins to head that way. But a warrior on a monstrous horse appeared from behind, nudging his horse between me and the camp. He did not look in my direction. His muscles bulged underneath his silver scale as he rode like the wind.

I became agitated and drew my jian to force my way through.

Without breaking stride he met my gaze, his blue eyes shining with the brightness of the sun.

I recognized the god and wished to sheathe my sword, but he shook his head and grinned. He spurred his scale-clad horse, and we entered the forest without slowing down.

The warrior placed a silver arrow on the string of his magnificent bow and drew back to his ear, aiming at the Gothic village, but at the last moment he wheeled his horse with his legs and released. The arrow flew back the way we came from.

I was confused, unsure of what to do.

Arash smiled then and took the reins of my horse. I let him, surrendering to his will.

I woke with a start. At peace.

The god of war and fire had spoken.

We struck camp early the next morning, heading north and east, towards the winter camp of the Roxolani.

For the first time in weeks we had a destination. We were not just running away from the killers of my father, we had a purpose.

After days on the road, our path crossed with a patrol of the Roxolani, led by none other than Elmanos.

We clasped arms. "Lord, king Bradakos is sick with worry. For you and for his adopted daughter." He looked at the little girl sitting on the horse in front of Gordas. "And you have brought his granddaughter."

Segelinde explained to Aritê that we were on our way to stay with her grandfather, but that we would visit with another grandfather along the way. My father had doted on her, so her expectation of a grandfather was firmly set in her mind.

I was not sure how Bradakos would react to the presence of Kniva, so when we came close to the camp, I left my companions to rest and rode with Elmanos to speak to the king.

On my arrival at the camp, I was escorted to the tent of the king without delay.

Bradakos was waiting outside and waved away his bodyguards' attempts to disarm me. He embraced me, clearly relieved to find me alive and well.

"Elmanos told me what had happened at Rhesaina in the aftermath of your victory", he said.

He handed me a silver cup filled with red wine. "Now tell me what happened since."

I told him all. How we rode for weeks to save my family, arriving less than a watch after the speculatores of Philip the Arab had attacked.

"We killed them all, Bradakos, but it was too late for Nik. A few of the assassins managed to gain entry into the compound. Nik saved my family, but he paid the ultimate price."

I could see the sadness rise in Bradakos. "He died as it befits a warrior. He is feasting with his friend Apsikal", he said, and pointed to the sky.

Bradakos drank deeply to dispel the sadness. "I will speak to Octar. You will stay with the Roxolani."

I shook my head. "It is not the will of Arash."

Bradakos looked at me quizzically, but held back his retort. He searched my face for any sign of deceit. After what felt like a watch, he nodded. "Just make sure you visit."

8

"There is one other thing, Bradakos", I said, and smiled awkwardly. "I have the iudex of the Thervingi waiting outside the camp."

Chapter 2 – Messenger

Exactly one moon after crossing the Danube we camped within a day's ride from the abode of the Thervingi Goths.

Gordas and his Huns remained with the Roxolani, and Thiaper went back to his people, the Carpiani.

Rodoulphos's mercenary warband was still camped close to the Thervingi fort and the big Heruli left to join his men.

I called an impromptu meeting with my companions to discuss our new life.

"Tomorrow we will arrive at our destination, the stronghold of the Thervingi, the people of Segelinde and Kniva. I have brought you to safety, but I will not keep you in these lands against your will. I would have your thoughts on this."

"To Hades with Rome", Hostilius said. "I burned my Roman clothes two days ago. All of it. I'm not going back."

Marcus scowled. "I was searching for my Roman garb this morning but I couldn't find it. I remember tying it to the packhorse, right next to yours, Primus Pilus."

Everyone stared at Hostilius, thinking the obvious. "What are you all looking at me for? Like I would have burned your clothes as well, Tribune!"

Following a few heartbeats of silence, he said: "Alright, alright, I may have and I'm sorry! It did seem like a large bundle. But I'm not saying it was me. Just that I might have."

Marcus held up his hand. "I was looking for it because I also wanted to burn mine."

It was Hostilius's turn to scowl.

"I have told you before, Lucius, it is not my wish to leave the Empire, but I have no choice", Marcus said.

I nodded.

Vibius said his bit: "I am staying with you, Lucius. Just for the record, I think my Roman clothes got mixed up with the Primus Pilus's." He held out a bundle to Hostilius. "I think this is yours, sir."

"I will use this experience to move closer to Dao", Cai interjected.

I was uncertain whether he referred to our exile or the clothes burning.

Pezhman was polishing sections of his complete set of armour that I gifted him as a reward for delivering the fake message to the Sasanians. At the time, Gordas looted the armour from an Immortal Guard who proved to be mortal. The magnificent set of armour was priceless, especially in the barbarian lands.

11

The ex-Persian scout did not even look up from his toil. "I go where you go, lord."

Felix and Egnatius had grown close since both retired from the legions a few years before, although the former still acted as though he was in active service.

Egnatius stood, saluted and said: "I understand Tribune, and I will obey."

I sighed and Felix smiled, tapping Egnatius on the back as he sat down.

"Umbra, I will keep looking after the horses, won't I?" Felix said. "As long as I have them, I am happy. Old Egnatius will give me a hand. Even Pezhman is handy around them." He winked at a grinning Pezhman.

I did not expect a reply from Adelgunde. She was returning home to her people as the babysitter of the niece of the iudex. Her biggest challenge would be to come to terms with the stellar rise in her social status.

Aritê was asleep next to Little Nik and Segelinde smiled, not wanting to wake her.

I nodded. "It is good then. You are all family to me. I have asked Arash for guidance. He will show us the way - of that I am certain."

I knew not that it would happen sooner than I expected.

Kniva's stint in Persia greatly enhanced his reputation. He was heralded as the returning hero by his people. Yet, he was away for long, and consequently had much to attend to. The Gothic iudex had to visit with his minor lords to judge disputes and reaffirm oaths of loyalty.

We all enjoyed the hospitality of my in-laws, but they understood that we could not live with them for ever. Kniva arranged for us to take possession of an empty complex which belonged to the would-be usurper, Werinbert, whom I had taken care of years earlier.

Kniva smiled. "It is fit that you live in the house vacated by my cousin, as you were the one who sent him across the river."

Our new accommodation proved spacious. It consisted of a main hall, a smaller hall for my hearth warriors, as well as staff quarters. Not to mention the many stables, with a large yard hemmed in by a palisade fence.

Segelinde and I moved into the large hall with Aritê. Marcus, Hostilius, Vibius and Cai would stay in the warrior hall and the others each had a large room of their own in the staff accommodation.

Little Nik was growing fast and although he was meant to live in the yard, he soon became fond of lying next to the hearth fire, close to Aritê, of course.

I expected the winter to be harsh, but to my surprise it was mild, with little snow or rain.

We were able to salvage the entire breeding herd, save one or two, in the aftermath of the attack on the farm. Felix and Egnatius immediately immersed themselves in caring for the horses, soon drawing in Pezhman as well. We cross-bred the Roman horses with the Hunnic horses and the Niseans with the aim to improve their endurance, hardiness and power.

While they played with the horses, Hostilius, Vibius, Marcus and I trained to improve our martial skills. Kniva's men had looted some fine Parthian bows in our recent war with the Sasanians and I had no trouble procuring one for each of my companions.

"Great shot, Primus Pilus", I said as Hostilius's arrow struck near the centre of the target.

"You know, Domitius, if I had known how easy it was, I would have looted a bow years ago."

"Try it when a Hun is galloping your way with his spear drawn back", I replied.

Hostilius scowled and released another arrow into the centre of the target.

While they practised with the bow, Cai tutored me in the way of the Dao. I was at a level where we trained specific movements in response to the actions of the opponent.

Cai raised his sword, held in both hands, above his right shoulder, ready to deliver an angled cut from high to low.

"When opponent go high, lower position. Receive blade with flat of sword. Send enemy away with same move, power come from legs."

He attacked in the same way.

"Meet blade, roll wrist, leave edge harmless. Move in with sweep, like harvest grain." He demonstrated. "Hit enemy with edge. Do not cut. Edge hit with power of thunder, destroying all inside."

Sometimes it would take weeks before the little man from Serica was content with the position of my feet, the elevation of my elbow or the angle of my blade. But I knew by then that he was a master at his craft and I endured.

I was bound by oath not to impart the techniques of the Dao. When I trained with my companions, I taught them the blade craft of the Huns and the Roxolani, who were masters in their own right.

Gordas made a small bow for Aritê and many days she would join us in practise. I was surprised at her natural ability. When

I extracted the arrows from the leather and straw target one day, I became concerned that the bow might be too well made as the arrows had penetrated the thick leather.

Slowly the season changed and winter made way for spring.

We honed our skills, worked with the horses, hunted and feasted. I was settling into my new life as a nobleman of the Goths. I was doing what Nik wanted me to do. I was following my destiny.

Or so I thought until late one summer afternoon.

Egnatius manned the gate and he came to call me. He saluted smartly, as in his own mind, he was still in the legions.

"At ease soldier", I said.

"Tribune, there is a barbarian at the gate, on a lathered horse. He is rambling incoherently. Should I chase him away?"

"He also seems to be wounded", Egnatius added as an afterthought.

I lit a torch with the flame from an oil lamp and briskly walked to the gate. The Thervingi warrior had fallen from his horse and was lying unconscious on the ground, bleeding from a wound to his upper arm.

We carried the injured man to the warrior hall and heartbeats later Cai joined us, carrying two leather pouches.

Cai cleaned the wound with vinegar and applied honey and a herb paste. He expertly bound it with a clean linen bandage, afterwards feeding the delirious warrior some or other secret herbal potion.

"He lost much blood. Only talk tomorrow", Cai said and left for his quarters.

Segelinde heard the commotion and came to investigate. "I know this man, he is called Ulfilas, a trusted hearth warrior of Kniva's."

She turned to me, suddenly worried. "We need to hear his message, Eochar. Kniva had left earlier with an escort of two hundred of his warriors to visit with his lords in the north. He is surely in some kind of predicament."

My wife and Adelgunde took charge. "We will watch over him, husband."

"Vibius, please help me move the bedroll closer to the fire", she commanded. "Marcus, I need water from the well."

I watched in amazement how the hardened soldiers obeyed my wife's every command.

Then Adelgunde turned to Hostilius. "Primus Pilus, we need some more wood for the fire."

Hostilius nodded and quickly returned with an armful of firewood.

17

My facial expression must have given me away. With a frown, Segelinde turned to me. "If you are going to mock me rather than help me, find something better to do."

Hostilius scowled and everyone stared at me with disapproval.

I returned his scowl and went to find Cai.

He was ready with advice. "Good general know when defeated. Best withdraw from battle when outnumbered."

Cai was cleaning and packing my weapons and armour.

He answered my quizzical look: "When clouds gather, soon rain fall. When messenger arrive wounded, soon we leave."

Chapter 3 – The Patient One

Ulfilas regained consciousness before the sun rose the following morning, just like Cai had predicted.

I had fallen asleep next to Aritê.

Adelgunde came to call me. When I entered the hall, Segelinde was assisting the messenger to sip some ale. His appearance was still ashen, but his condition had improved markedly.

He inclined his head to Segelinde and me. "I thank you for keeping me alive."

Segelinde nodded in acknowledgement.

Ulfilas told his tale.

"The iudex was on his way to visit his northern lords. Two hundred of us, his oathsworn, accompanied him. We were on our way to Lord Adosinda, whose lands border those of the Venedi." He spat out the word 'Venedi'.

"Not five miles from the stronghold of Lord Adosinda we were ambushed by a large warband. Half of the oathsworn were killed. The rest of us, who survived, fought to save the life of the iudex. We fought as we retreated, eventually reaching the abode of the lord. The Venedi surrounded the fort with many hundreds of warriors."

He drank again to wet his throat. "I evaded the Venedi when night fell and stole two of their horses." A smile touched his lips as he recalled the small act of vengeance.

He shook his head slowly. "Teiwaz guided me as I slowly picked my way through the forest, but at first light, Lok played his tricks. I stumbled upon a clearing occupied by three Fennians."

"What are Fennians?" Marcus asked in his broken Goth.

"Fennians are the closest a man can come to being an animal, without actually being one", Ulfilas replied with disgust.

"At first I thought that I had stumbled upon wolves feasting on a kill, but in the dim light one creature rose on its hind legs. Without hesitating I jerked the reins to avoid them, but one cast his axe before I was sheltered by the trees." He gestured towards his wound. "If I had not moved, the axe would have split my skull."

"I rode for three days and three nights, only resting when the horses could no more."

He met my gaze. "Lord Eochar, the iudex requests that you visit him."

His message confused me, but Segelinde came to the rescue. "You have honoured your oath, Ulfilas son of Helyas. Rest now, you will be rewarded."

"Thank you, Princess", he said and laid back down, exhausted by the exertion.

She took me by the arm and led me away to my companions. She spoke in Latin. "I fear for my brother. He is in trouble, but he will not openly ask for help. It would show weakness. There are many Goth lords who wait in the shadows, ready to seize power."

"Rodoulphos will surely help", I said, "but there are only a thousand under his command."

"Is it not possible to ask his father-in-law, Ostrogotha the Patient, for assistance?" Marcus asked.

"Let me speak with Kniva's wife", Segelinde suggested.

While we waited for Segelinde, Hostilius asked: "Do you know why they call him 'The Patient'?

"Patience is good virtue", Cai added. "He must be wise and benevolent king."

Segelinde soon returned. "She agrees with our plan, but said that her father is not an easy man to deal with."

21

"Is he not known for his patience? How difficult can it be to go speak to a patient king?" Hostilius said.

"Why do they call him that?" he asked as an afterthought.

"Primus Pilus, I was told a tale that when he was but ten summers old, a warrior, a Goth champion, offended him. In which way, I do not know. Ostrogotha did not seek vengeance, knowing that he was no match for the older champion. Yet he did not forget, neither did he forgive."

"Ten years went by and Ostrogotha became a man. Only then did he challenge the champion to single combat. He inflicted terrible wounds on the warrior, but did not kill him. He patiently waited and guarded the body for a full day, allowing the man to die in agony. That is how he was given his nickname."

"Bloody misleading", Hostilius mumbled.

I immediately headed for the camp of the Heruli.

I found Rodoulphos sitting outside his tent. A few wild fowl were grilling over a slow fire while he shared ale with his comrades. He smiled when he saw me approach and raised his ale horn.

"What message does Teiwaz have for the Master of the Runes?" the Heruli chieftain asked.

I smiled. "I carry an urgent message from the war god, indeed."

The big Erilaz of the Heruli motioned for me to take a seat vacated by an underling.

I explained all. "I suggest we ride north, to the border of the lands of the Greuthungi. I will then ride to Ostrogotha, to request his assistance."

He waved away my suggestion with a grin. "Ostrogotha is a difficult bastard, but fortunately for us, I know the bastard well. The warriors of the Heruli have fought for him many times."

He took a long swig from his horn and wiped his dripping beard with the back of his hand. "I will ride with you. But be warned, he is not one who gives without receiving. He will want something in return."

I spent the evening with Segelinde and my father-in-law, Hildebald.

"The Heruli chieftain is right, Eochar", Hildebald said. "I suggest you pledge Kniva's future assistance to the Greuthungi. You will need to make haste. I do believe Kniva is in much danger."

I spent a fitful night worrying about what I was getting myself into. The ways of the Goths were largely unknown to me, but I had no choice. Arash had taken the reins.

Cai agreed to stay at home with Segelinde and Aritê. I left the following morning with Hostilius, Marcus, Vibius and the thousand-strong warband of Heruli.

It took three days to reach the borderlands of the Greuthungi. Rodoulphos and ten of his oathsworn rode with me to find the king. On the second day we were intercepted by a Greuthungi patrol. They recognized the Heruli leader and we were escorted to the stronghold of Ostrogotha.

The Greuthungi dwelled north and west of the Dark Sea, on the Sea of Grass. Unlike the Scythians, they lived mostly in one place.

We approached the hillfort through a wide, flat river valley. Many hundreds of sunken-floor dwellings lined the western bank. Sheep, horses and cattle grazed in small groups, watched over by wide-eyed herdboys. The track meandered through the settlement and rose towards the stronghold on the hill. The flat crest of the hill was unfortified, but the rocky landscape made the hill inaccessible to horsemen, except for where the track passed through the gated fissure. Rodoulphos rode forward to gain us entrance, while I studied the defences. It would be difficult for men on foot to scale the rocky cliffs, but impossible for horsemen. On the Sea of Grass, the danger came from horsemen. The Goths had chosen well.

Rodoulphos and I were escorted into the stronghold, while the Heruli's oathsworn remained in the company of the guards. It was clear that the Greuthungi knew the mercenary well.

The path rose gently and led to a flat piece of ground occupied by three wooden halls. I assumed that the large hall belonged to the king, but I was mistaken. We rounded the corner to the smallest of the three. In front of the hall, at least fifteen warriors were engaged in training with the sword. One of the men was older than the rest, his beard streaked with strands of grey.

The king was of medium height, yet so broad in the shoulders that it gave him an awkward appearance. His shoulders and neck were heavily muscled, which spoke of countless hours of sparring with a heavy blade. Despite his age, he appeared no less fit or lacking in ability. In fact, he bested the younger sparring partner, a tall, muscular warrior at least ten years his junior.

King Ostrogotha clasped the arm of the warrior, signalling the end of the training. He removed his simple, yet well-made, iron helmet. Blonde braided hair fell to his shoulders.

He sheathed his longsword - a magnificent weapon. Where the Thervingi favoured the spear, I had heard that the Greuthungi were fond of the double-edged longsword.

Flanked by his oathsworn, the king strolled towards us. Both Rodoulphos and I went down on one knee, inclining our heads as a sign of respect.

"Prince Eochar of the Roxolani, is it not?" he asked.

We remained as we were, as he had not given us permission to rise.

"Yes, lord", I replied.

"I hear that Bradakos of the Roxolani is fond of you, the Heruli revere you, Octar of the Urugundi fears you, but Philip Caesar wishes you dead?"

"Yes, lord."

"My son-in-law desires my assistance and you have come to ask me for it?"

"Yes, lord."

"Come", he said, walking back to the training area. He discreetly nodded to a guard who returned my sword. As I was not wearing a helmet, he threw his to a guard. He drew his sword.

I was not ignorant enough to draw my jian. It is not allowed to draw your sword in the presence of a king without permission. I did not even allow my hand to rest on the hilt.

"Draw", he said, and raised his sword in a two handed grip above his left shoulder. He stepped in, striking an immensely powerful vertical blow from left to right.

My sword was free in a flash. I lunged forward and to the right, lowering the position of my body. I held my jian above my head, the tip pointing backwards with the blade angled towards the ground. His blade slid off the flat of my sword, not finding any opposition, unbalancing him. As his sword cleared mine, I stepped forward again, rising to my full height. I was perfectly positioned to dispatch him, as my sword was drawn back and his body was open to a strike.

I returned to a simple guard position.

Ostrogotha sheathed his longsword and narrowed his eyes. "They call you 'Eochar the Merciless', yet you did not strike", he said.

I grinned, "And they call you 'Ostrogotha the Patient', lord, yet you struck with the speed of a viper."

Rodoulphos interjected. "Hygelac, the greatest champion of the Heruli, did not last a hundred heartbeats against Eochar.

The magic of Hygelac was strong, yet it helped him naught. Prince Eochar walks with Teiwaz, of that I am sure."

Ostrogotha nodded. He gestured for the Heruli to follow him. "Come, walk with me, Prince Eochar. You and the Heruli will share a horn of ale with me while we talk."

He led us into the hall where a roaring fire was blazing in the hearth. An abundance of soft furs were scattered around the fire and he motioned for us to sit. He sat down on a low bench and a servant girl brought us horns filled to the brim.

In the veins of the king flowed the royal blood of the Amalings, the descendants of Teiwaz. He was supremely confident and not one to mince his words or waste his breath on small talk.

"Prince Eochar, I will not leave the husband of my daughter to die at the hands of the northern savages", Ostrogotha said. "A thousand of my horse warriors will join the Heruli. I cannot spare you more, as we are engaged in brutal conflict with the Alani to the east. In return, I will accept your pledge of assistance on behalf of the Thervingi Goths."

"I make that pledge on behalf of Kniva, lord", I replied.

"I require your personal pledge as well, Prince Eochar. You are here with me, not Kniva."

Ostrogotha was not only a fearsome warrior and leader of men. He possessed cunning. I could not withhold my pledge, for the sake of my wife's family.

I could feel the hands of Arash tightening on the reins.

Resigned to my fate, I said: "I give you my pledge of assistance."

Ostrogotha visibly relaxed and he smiled for the first time since I have met him. "Our new alliance calls for a celebration. We will feast tonight."

Chapter 4 – Venedi

On the morn of the second day following the feast, Rodoulphos and I departed from the stronghold of the Amaling king with one thousand mounted Goths at our back.

It was clear that the Greuthungi had benefited from centuries of subduing and fighting the Scythian and Sarmatian tribes. For one, they were excellent horsemen, unlike the Thervingi. The men were generally taller and leaner with some clearly displaying their Scythian heritage in their facial features. I am sure some of the men were purebred Alans, although I could not be certain.

Ostrogotha entrusted his men to a general named Guntharic, subject to my command.

We spent two full days on the road. Early in the morning on the third day, we sent a messenger ahead to warn the Heruli of our imminent arrival later in the day. The warband of the Greuthungi rode into the Heruli camp during the third watch, with Rodoulphos, Guntharic and me at the head of the column.

As arranged by Rodoulphos, the Heruli warriors were ready to ride. At dusk I called a halt. We made camp, and my companions and I joined Rodoulphos and Guntharic around a blazing fire. While a deer was slowly roasting over a spit, we drank ale and made plans.

The Heruli pointed west and north. "There lie the lands of Adosinda the Goth. We will cross into his lands just after the sun rises tomorrow. Thirty Roman miles from here we will find his stronghold."

"Do you have men who know this area?" I asked.

The Erilaz grinned. "I have sent them already. They are wolf warriors, shape-shifters with strong magic. They wear skins and keep to the shadows."

He drank deeply from his horn. "The scouts will meet us tomorrow, ten miles from the fort. We will know the numbers of the enemy."

"Tell me about the Venedi and the Fenni", I said.

Guntharic was the one who replied. "The Venedi are known for their kindness towards travellers. When they feel that they have been wronged, they will strike back with a vengeance." He looked at me and Rodoulphos in turn, implying that somehow the barbarians had been wronged.

He drank and continued. "The Venedi are a numerous and hardy race divided into a multitude of tribes ruled by minor kings. Some have taken to the ways of the Scythians and breed horses, but most live in the forests along the banks of rivers."

31

"It is not advisable to do battle with them in the woods. They are swift and know their way around the forests. They carry short javelins and oversized shields. Some tribes carry primitive wooden bows with short arrows."

My comrades had a good grasp of the language and Hostilius sighed a sigh of relief. "At least the arrows can't hurt us. I hate arrows."

Guntharic grinned. "Do not be put at ease, Roman. They smear the wooden arrows with an evil potion. It is said that they have acquired the formula from the Scythians."

I frowned, but my companions stared at him blankly.

"I know of this", I said. "It is called Scythicon. Many generations ago, a tribe far to the north and east, the Irycai, is said to have been given the recipe by Tapio, the spirit of the forest. Because of its potency, the secret is only known to the royalty and the most senior of shamans among my people."

"In the culture of the Scythians, a man may only use this against an enemy if he has been wronged in an evil way. The king has to give his permission."

Hostilius asked me outright. "You are a prince. Do you know how it is made?"

I nodded. "I am oathbound not to share the method, but I will enlighten you. It is a blend of snake venom, human blood, dung and rotten flesh."

He pressed on. "What happens when one is injured by such an arrow?"

"You start shivering within heartbeats", I continued. "Then you vomit bile while the blood that seeps from the wound turns black and frothy. Not unlike this ale."

Hostilius swallowed, a slow scowl of disgust appearing on his face.

"If that doesn't kill you", I added, "the green rot that sets in will."

"The warriors of the Venedi are most vulnerable when they are caught in the open, or surprised", Guntharic said. "They are familiar with the forest, so they will try to lure us into the dense trees or ambush us in a wooded area."

"And the Fenni?" I asked.

"They live in the wild, as savage and base as animals. Furs are worn as clothing and they have no home apart from crude shelters woven from branches. Their main weapon is the battle-axe which they use in war and on the hunt. I have witnessed an axe kill a warrior at a range of forty paces. Some carry enormous wooden hunting bows, as tall as a man. The arrows are tipped with bone, not iron, but they are heavy and kill easily."

I looked towards Rodoulphos for advice, as he was familiar with the area. "Do we have to travel through a forested area where there is danger of an ambush?"

He nodded, smiling evilly, and I shared my plan.

We left early the following morning. Before the sun rose over the hills, we had forded the shallow river that marked the boundary of the lands of Adosinda.

Hostilius rode at my side at the head of a column of five hundred Heruli. The landscape was shrubby, as was to be expected of this area where the Sea of Grass slowly gave way to the dense northern forests. Visibility was good on both sides of the track and we rode at a slow canter without fear of an ambush.

There was no sign of the returning Heruli scouts.

We spotted dense trees in the distance two thirds of a watch later, having placed at least twenty miles between us and the overnight camp.

All the warriors in the column wore full armour and their shields were held at the ready. Hostilius and I had brought our Roman issue legionary scuta. The large rectangular shields would serve us well.

As arranged, we increased our pace as we entered the shadows cast by the huge oaks.

The road straightened after we had travelled a quarter of a mile into the forest. In the distance I recognized the Heruli scouts.

Their heads were prominently displayed on the hafts of spears rammed into the centre of the roadway.

As one we reined in our horses and dismounted. We formed a wall of shields on either side of the track with the horses in the centre. On the sides of the road we could see movement among the trees, the shapes illuminated by the shivelights.

Slowly we began to walk back the way we came.

The forest suddenly came to life as hundreds of screaming savages burst from the trees.

The men with us were the best of the Heruli. Big, powerful warriors who could wield the terrible broad-bladed battle-axe single-handed. In contrast to our heavily armoured warriors, the enemy wore little protection apart from furs.

A throwing axe embedded itself in my shield, followed a heartbeat later by a heavy arrow issued from a Fenni bow. To my surprise, the arrow struck with such force that the bone-tipped missile pierced the shield and protruded an inch on the inside.

Then they were upon us. A warrior wielding a long-hafted axe jumped into the air while his weapon moved downward in an overhead strike. I stepped forward, using the shield offensively. The metal boss of the shield struck him squarely in the face. He fell unconscious and Hostilius dispatched him with a quick downward strike of his gladius.

A short, dark-haired warrior ran at me, his shoulder lowered, with the intention of tipping over my shield. I tilted my scutum sideways and swung my gladius from low to high, removing one side of his unprotected head in the process.

A giant clad in furs used the opportunity to throw his axe. I barely had time to deflect the weapon with the rim of my shield. He rammed his spear at my face with viper-like speed. I turned my head and the blade scored a line along my helmet. As he ran into my shield, I stepped backwards and he stumbled. I lowered my shield and thrust the tip of my gladius into his eye. I stepped over the corpse, closing the line again, just in time to dispatch a young warrior too eager to take my armour as plunder.

As quickly as it had started, the attack ended.

I gave the signal and at least ten horses without riders, but with swords tied to the saddles, were sent into the forest by a slap of a blade on the rump. In order to catch wild animals, bait was needed.

We continued our slow retreat. Half of the Heruli warriors lay draped over their horses, feigning injury. Every so often, a horse was released into the undergrowth, resulting in screams of pleasure as the barbarians claimed the priceless horses and even scarcer iron weapons.

Hostilius whispered under his breath. "It looks like your plan is working, Domitius. The whole bloody forest is crawling with savages."

By the time we exited the woods, the barbarians had worked themselves into a frenzy. We had baited them with another ten horses loaded with iron weapons and mail armour. Only a hundred of the Heruli were still walking. The rest were draped over their horses or sat slumped in their saddles.

When our group came to a halt two hundred paces from the woods on the flat plain, it was too much for the savages to bear. Only one hundred fit men stood between them and the priceless loot of five hundred horses and an abundance of weapons and armour.

They ran at us from the woods, numbering at least two thousand. It was what I had been waiting for. A grinning Heruli signalled with his horn and one and a half thousand Greuthungi and Heruli horsemen charged from where they were concealed in the undergrowth, two hundred paces from the track.

The 'injured' Heruli warriors miraculously healed and all mounted. Our numbers were now equal to that of the barbarians, but the forest dwelling savages were no match for the heavily armed and armoured horsemen of the Goths and the Heruli.

The Venedi and Fenni froze, and sealed their fate in the process. Hundreds fell as the wall of horses crashed through their lines and trampled them into the dust.

Some of the enemy managed to escape back to the forest, but most were cut off from the sanctuary of the trees.

We surrounded the milling mass of disorganized men.

I leaped from the horse when the signifier blew a deafening note on his horn. I shouted in my best parade ground voice, speaking in Scythian. "Who speaks for you? Come forward!"

All went quiet and reluctantly a warrior moved towards me, men parting to let him pass through. His clothing was indistinguishable from the rest, yet he carried himself with dignity. His hair and beard was dark, which matched his eyes.

"What you want, Goth?" he said in passable Scythian and spat in the dirt.

I removed my helmet. "I am no Goth. I am Eochar of the Roxolani", I said in my friendliest tone.

He narrowed his eyes and said: "I am Vlad."

I motioned for him to follow me and we walked thirty paces distant, out of earshot of the men.

"Why have you attacked us, Vlad?"

He smirked. "What it to you, Scythian dog of Goths?"

I was losing patience with the savage. My hand went to my sword and there was iron in my tone. "Vlad of the Venedi. Measure your next words carefully as it will determine your fate and that of your people."

"I ask you again, for the last time. Why have you attacked us?"

He knew that the time for posturing was at an end. The Venedi rubbed his eyes and his fingers settled on the bridge of his nose. He sighed and kept his eyes closed. The actions of a man resigned to his fate.

Vlad the Venedi shared his tale in broken Scythian.

"A moon ago, traders from Venedi and Fenni travel to talk with Lord Adosinda, the Goth. The tribes have desire to trade with Goths. They also want trade with strange war-like people who live other side of Mother River. They called Romani."

He was pointing to the south so I assumed he referred to the Danube and the lands of Rome.

Vlad continued. "Traders never return. I go speak with Lord Adosinda. He said traders killed by Goth king. Adosinda feel sad about traders but he fears powerful, evil Goth king."

Vlad hit his chest with his fist. "I say to Adosinda that Venedi not afraid of king. Only evil man kills innocent travellers. Adosinda tell us when Goth king come. We wait and try to kill evil man, but he hides with Adosinda."

Vlad grinned then. "But Lord Adosinda sent messenger. He said that tonight, he leave small gate open in wall. We kill evil king. Everyone happy then. Vlad take his people and go home."

"Yes, Vlad", I replied. "Everyone will be happy, especially Lord Adosinda. Once you have killed the king, Adosinda will kill you. Then he will be the one who has avenged the king. Soon he will make a move on the throne as well, after he has taken your lands and killed your people."

I could see that I had planted a seed of doubt in his mind, but he was not convinced, so I pushed my advantage.

"Your warriors will remain under guard of my men, while two of us go with you tonight, to kill the Goth king."

He frowned then, confused.

I grinned and explained.

Chapter 5 – Assassins

I discarded my Scythian armour in exchange for clothes of the Fenni, looted from the dead.

I wore primitive braccae of deer hide and a short-sleeved bearskin jerkin with the fur on the inside. And I started to itch immediately after donning the musty skins. I tried to put the newly acquired infestation from my mind, focusing on the task at hand.

"Why does Hostilius get to join you, Lucius?" asked Vibius, clearly dejected. Marcus wore a similar expression.

"He blends in the best", I said while trying to get my feet into the mouldy deerskin boots.

"What do you mean by 'blends in', Domitius?" Hostilius asked while narrowing his eyes.

Hostilius had grown his beard and shaved his head, looking every bit as savage as the average Fenni.

"I mean it as a compliment, Primus Pilus. You know how to act the part, like the Greek actors of old", I replied.

"Are you calling me a Greek now?" he said and scowled.

I held up both hands with palms open. "Peace, Primus Pilus. I mean to say that I need a killer by my side."

He grinned, placated by my words, and carried on tying the fur leg wrapping in place.

Hostilius wore a knitted wool tunic which had at least a couple of previous owners, with the skin of an enormous wolf draped over it all like a cloak.

He sniffed the skin and pulled up his nose. "It smells like, like... "

"Fox piss", I interjected. "It's an old hunter's trick to mask the smell of a man." Hostilius regarded the fur as if its previous owner was a leper, so I added: "Sometimes they use the excrement as well."

Vlad had told us earlier that a thousand of his men were still encamped around the fortress to ensure that the evil king did not escape. Within the walls, many huts and halls surrounded the compound of the king. Kniva and ten of his oathsworn were housed in a separate hall, as befitted their status.

We waited patiently until darkness descended, then departed for the stronghold of Lord Adosinda.

We rode in the middle of the road, in full view. We did not fear an attack as Vlad had sent word of our imminent arrival. Close to the hillfort we were challenged by sentries set by the Venedi. Vlad muttered words of which I did not know the meaning, and we dismounted on his signal.

42

"We walk from here. My men will look after horses", Vlad said.

Hostilius and I followed obediently. We walked uphill, stumbling repeatedly. Fortunately our eyes became accustomed to the darkness and soon we noticed the walls of the fort silhouetted against the sky.

Vlad went to ground, crouching behind a small bush, and hooted like an owl. He repeated the call thrice.

Within heartbeats we heard the creaking of a seldom-used door being opened. We followed the Venedi to the black doorway where a hulking Gothic warrior waited.

"I told you that only one man must come, Vlad of the Venedi", the man hissed. "Send them away!"

"They are family of the wrongfully slain, lord", Vlad countered. "They are merchants, but they have sworn an oath of vengeance. We can only return home once they have fulfilled their oath."

The brooding figure growled: "Since when is an oath important to the Venedi?"

Vlad offered no reply and a couple of heartbeats passed in silence. The big man sighed. "Bring them, then. It matters not."

The Goth led us along an uneven dirt path that meandered through clusters of huts. More than once my boot slipped on something that had an all too familiar consistency. The snoring of the warriors inside were the only sounds as we passed the low doorways.

We must have walked two hundred paces when the shadows of the huts on both sides of the path gave way to a large open space.

The Goth allowed us to catch up to him. He walked a few paces to the left and crouched behind the corner of a hall, where we joined him.

He whispered: "The evil one is inside this hall. He is the only one sleeping on the raised portion on the far side. The door is around the corner. I will wait close by. Be careful, there is a sentry outside the door." With that, he backtracked and disappeared, no doubt to ready his warriors to slaughter us after we had done his dirty work. He would then claim to have avenged the iudex.

With my one hand resting on the crude cut oak post for balance, I crouched and whispered: "Wait for my signal."

I slowly crept up to the corner of the hall, lay down flat on my stomach, and inched forward. I stole a peek around the corner. On the steps sat a warrior, staring forward into the darkness.

I inched back and came to a crouch, feeling around the base of the corner post for a small pebble. Once I found what I was looking for, I peeked again, still crouching. The guard was still in the same position.

I offered a quick prayer to Arash and Fortuna and from around the corner of the hall, threw the stone high over the roof, hoping that it would fall somewhere on the far side of the guard.

I crouched and peeked, all the muscles in my body tight as a bowstring.

Fortuna favoured me, and the stone landed on the far side of the guard with a soft but audible impact.

He stood and turned towards the direction of the sound, suddenly alert. I covered the ten paces swiftly and silently, rose behind him and clamped my left hand around his mouth in a grip of iron. I hit him with the heel of my right hand palm where his neck supported his skull, just as Cai had taught me. He slumped, unconscious. I dragged him around the corner to where Hostilius and Vlad were waiting.

Hostilius nodded. Vlad regarded me with wide eyes.

I motioned and they followed me through the doorway into the hall.

The only light was provided by the glowing coals in the large hearth. We carefully shuffled along the wall, trying our utmost not to disturb the snoring oathsworn of the iudex.

I spotted Kniva close to the hearth on the raised platform on the far side of the hall. Hostilius and Vlad crouched in the shadows while I crept forward. When I was but three paces from my brother-in-law, a warrior near me sat up and rubbed his eyes. I lay down, as if I had passed out earlier. He stood, half-tripped over me and swore under his breath. My hand tightened around my dagger, but he moved on, disappearing outside. I had to act quickly, as he would surely notice the absence of the guard. I motioned with my head and Hositilius moved towards the doorway, in case the sleepy warrior returned and tried to raise the alarm.

I lay down beside Kniva, accidentally bumping him with my elbow. He stirred and as he opened his eyes I clamped my hand over his mouth.

"Be quiet", I hissed, "we are all in mortal danger."

He blinked a couple of times and then nodded. I removed my hand.

Just then the warrior returned from making water. He looked around in panic, but as he was about to shout the alarm, Hostilius silenced him by hitting him on the temple with the hilt of his dagger. He caught the slumping warrior mid-air and gently lay him on the ground.

Kniva watched in amazement.

I motioned for Vlad to join us.

"Adosinda started this war and blamed you for it", I whispered. "He has arranged for the Fenni to kill you this night. The traitor is waiting outside with his warriors and they mean to kill us. He thinks Hostilius and I are savages, like Vlad here."

Unsurprisingly, Vlad scowled.

I produced a small skin filled with fresh blood I hoped belonged to an unfortunate pig, earlier killed by the Venedi. I poured the already thick blood over my hands and dagger and gave Vlad a similar treatment.

I spoke to Kniva. "Rouse your men in silence, brother. When you hear the clash of blades, come to our assistance." He nodded, and while he quietly woke his men, I moved towards the door.

My Roman gladius was in my right hand and my dagger in the left. I noticed that Hostilius was armed the same way. Vlad led the way. He carried a dagger and an axe, of course.

Adosinda waited around the corner. Alone.

His gaze drifted towards our blood-smeared hands. The Goth lord had great difficulty hiding his joy.

Vlad spoke first. "Evil king is dead." He gestured towards us. "They have fulfilled their oaths. Venedi and Fenni go home now."

Behind Adosinda six men appeared from the shadows. These must have been his most trusted men. Men who would lie for him.

The Goth lord grinned. "You have served your purpose, stupid savages…"

And that was as far as he got. I had heard enough. There was no reason to delay the inevitable.

My gladius entered his throat, cutting into his spine as I struck like lightning. Before the Goths could react, Vlad's axe split the skull of the closest warrior while Hostilius buried his gladius in the gut of a third. A short warrior lunged at me. I blocked and severed his sword hand in the same movement. Another wielded a spear, I deflected the thrust and pulled on the shaft, running the razor edge of my blade across his throat as I passed him.

Hostilius dealt with his opponent. I heard a dull thud as the last man collapsed with a crude Fenni axe embedded in his forehead.

Kniva appeared from around the corner. For a moment he stared at the bodies littering the ground. "I didn't think you'd need my help, brother."

Kniva held out his arm and Vlad was wise to clasp it. "I will speak to you later, Vlad of the Venedi. Wait for me outside the walls."

He turned to me. "I will sort out this mess, then I will join you."

I was about to protest but he silenced me with a wave of his hand. "I have come to understand politics, my friend. Fear not. I will see you shortly."

Then he added as an afterthought: "If I were you, I would burn those clothes. The people of the Fenni are notorious for the variety of vermin that infest their person, and... something smells like piss."

Chapter 6 – Dragontooth

We went for a swim in the river after tossing the borrowed clothes into the fire. Hostilius smelled better, but it helped naught with the vermin.

A number of warriors offered foolproof remedies and soon we were ushered into a tent with a small fire lit in the centre. Ox dung and horse hairs were added and I almost choked to death from the acrid smoke. Then we were sponged down with vinegar and our beards and hair coated with olive oil.

I discovered that the lice of the Fenni were just as hardy as their hosts, finding several of the little critters still very much alive when we cleaned our hair and beards with a fine comb.

We were rescued from further ministrations by a messenger summoning us to the Gothic fort.

"I'd rather live with the vermin than inhale that bloody smoke again", Hostilius said, and pulled a louse from his beard, squashing it in the process.

"I agree, Primus Pilus", I replied, scratching my oily scalp.

We soon arrived at the stronghold of the Goth lord. Vlad, Rodoulphos and Guntharic were awaiting our arrival.

We clasped arms, and one of Kniva's men led us to the hall of the recently deceased Lord Adosinda.

Everything was seemingly back to normal. The townsfolk and warriors went about their business without affording us a second glance as we strode to the hall.

Entering into the presence of the king, all went down on one knee, except Vlad, who was also a king of his people. Kniva waved it away. He pointed to a heap of mail and weapons stacked neatly in the corner of the hall. "It is a gift to you, King Vlad of the Venedi, twenty chain mail jerkins, twenty swords and twenty helmets. All of good quality."

He gestured to an oathsworn, who handed Vlad a small chest. The Venedi opened it, revealing gold coins. By this time Vlad could hardly believe his good fortune, smiling from ear to ear.

Vlad was a king in his own way, but not nearly as powerful as the iudex of the mighty Thervingi. Yet, his station was recognised so he spoke. "My people will have peace with the Thervingi, King Kniva. We will trade and prosper."

Kniva nodded in recognition of his words. "Go with the gods, King Vlad. Our people will have peace. The Heruli will escort you home to ensure your safety."

We clasped arms with Vlad, bidding him farewell. The wild king of the swamps left with his newfound wealth. He would take his people home.

When he was out of earshot, Kniva said: "I don't trust the Venedi, nor the Fenni. Rodoulphos, make sure they don't raid Gothic settlements on their way home." The big Heruli nodded and left to attend to his appointed task.

Kniva turned to the Greuthungi war leader. "I am grateful to my father-in-law for his assistance, Guntharic."

Kniva grinned, then sighed deeply. "And I am sure that you had to provide payment in kind, Eochar. What oath did you give on my behalf?"

Since we were in the presence of his underlings as well as the Greuthungi, I replied formally. "Lord Kniva, I had to pledge your assistance in return, should it be called on by Lord Ostrogotha."

"Is that all?"

"No, lord, I had to provide my own oath of assistance as well", I replied.

He frowned then, looking at Guntharic, who shifted uncomfortably. "Lord Ostrogotha is a wise man. He recognises Lord Eochar's, er... talents. He believes that Lord Eochar walks with Teiwaz."

He nodded. "Leave us, Guntharic of the Greuthingi. You have done well. We will feast tonight, then all depart on the morrow."

The big Goth inclined his scarred head, his blonde braids falling around his armoured shoulders. He turned on his heel and left.

"Primus Pilus Hostilius", Kniva said. "As always, you were in the thick of the action. Not only are you a formidable hunter, but your name is spoken with fear and respect in the halls of the Goths. You have become a man of reputation."

Hostilius rarely grinned, but he did so then.

He spoke passable Goth and said: "Thank you, lord. You are not so bad for Goth as well."

Coming from anybody else, it would have been a huge insult to the Gothic iudex, but he knew the ironhard Primus Pilus well and recognised the compliment, which was rarely issued.

"I am honoured by your words, Primus Pilus", Kniva replied.

The king produced a vicious-looking dagger with an ivory handle. The blade was pattern-welded and contained strange writing symbols, the ancient magic runes of the gods. "This is the dagger that belonged to Adosinda. It is said to have been made by the dwarfs of Svartalfheim. It was brought to this land by my ancestors, from the ice islands of the north. It is called Dragontooth. Now it is yours."

Hostilius was visibly moved. He nodded, reverently accepting the dagger, handling it like a mother would a babe.

"Leave us now, Primus Pilus", he said. Hostilius left with a grin, eager to play with his new toy.

On Kniva's signal, an oathsworn warrior handed us both a horn of ale. His men left the hall to afford us the chance to speak in private.

"Adosinda broke his oath to me", Kniva said. "Sadly, it cost him his life and that of his family."

I nodded. It was brutal, but it was the way of the Goths.

"You did well, brother", he continued. "I was foolish not to suspect a plot. Adosinda had sent most of his warriors north and east nearly a moon ago to investigate so-called incursions into his lands. He did it deliberately, to enable the savages to trap us in this fort. I admit, it was a clever ploy."

"Fortuna was on our side, Kniva, else I would never have discovered the plot."

He grinned his boyish grin. "I think that it was Teiwaz."

We spoke and drank ale for a full watch while lounging on the furs next to the hearth fire.

Before I departed he said: "I need to appoint a new lord and receive the oaths of the warriors who are yet to return. You should return to my sister and enjoy your family. I owe you much."

"Brother, you rode with me when the Arab killed my father. You gave me sanctuary. You owe me naught", I replied.

I clasped his arm and returned to my comrades, eager to go home.

Chapter 7 – Golden flowers

Marcus and Vibius had each received a magnificent Gothic longsword from Kniva as a gesture of his appreciation. The swords were tied to their saddles.

Hostilius smirked. "Cheap bloody pieces of iron. That's all they are."

He drew his dagger from the ornate scabbard he had somehow managed to acquire. "Now this is a work of art. Not some iron slab beat flat by half-drunk barbarians."

Marcus scowled, but Vibius was curious. "What do the markings on the blade mean, Primus Pilus?"

"How in Hades should I know, Decurion? Do I look like a bloody Heruli?"

He did resemble the Heruli and I was sure that Vibius was about to point it out to Hostilius, so I felt compelled to interject, in order to keep the peace. "It reads 'I am the blade of Teiwaz'", I lied.

Hostilius smirked, now satisfied, while Marcus rolled his eyes. Kniva had told me that the dagger was indeed ancient and revered, but the inscription meant 'the one who tries'.

It was Marcus who changed the subject.

"What would you do if the Goths called on your oath of assistance?"

"I would honour my oath, of course", I replied.

"And what if they campaign against Rome?"

I answered with a question. "Rome murdered my father. Rome tried to kill us. Rome sent us away after we saved them from defeat against the Sasanians at Rhesaina. In our hour of need, Kniva helped us by giving us sanctuary. Would you not fight for the Goths against the people who had wronged us?"

He offered no answer. Not for a while, at least.

"I do not believe that the people of Rome wronged us", Marcus said. "I lay the blame at the feet of Philip the Arab and his despicable brother."

I wanted to answer, but he was not done and he held up his hand. "Yes, I would fight for Kniva against the Arab, not for the Goths against Rome."

"Is it not the same?"

I could see that this was a serious issue for Marcus. "For me, it is not the same", he said. "It is how I would be able to live with myself."

I understood.

"Marcus, it is but talk. Rome and the Goths have an agreement, a treaty of peace. The Goths get paid an annual tribute. They will not break their agreement. Even the Arab would not be that stupid."

That was what I thought at the time. I was soon to be proven wrong.

* * *

We arrived at our new home four days after leaving the former lands of Adosinda the Goth.

Egnatius's eye appeared in the peep-hole in the gate. A heartbeat later the gate swung open and as always, the oldster came to attention.

"Welcome home, Tribunes. Welcome Primus Pilus, Decurion", he said and saluted smartly.

"At ease, legionary", I said, now used to the roleplay.

We rounded the corner where Aritê came running to me with Little Nik hot on her heels. I noticed that Little Nik was not that little anymore as I scooped up my daughter in an embrace. The wolf growled, eyeing me with suspicion.

"Little Nik missed you a lot", she said, although I doubted it, based on his demeanour. His growl deepened, so I put her down. It proved to be effective, as Little Nik relaxed immediately.

"I missed you too, Aritê. Let's go find your mother." She pulled me towards the hall by my hand. The wolf seemed to have made peace with my presence and was sniffing my boots.

Segelinde appeared in the doorway of the hall. She ran to me and I hugged her close, lifting her from her feet. The wolf growled.

"No, Little Nik", was all she had to say to stop the growling. He skulked away and lay down at her feet.

"Your brother is well, which is more than I can say for the conniving Lord Adosinda", I said.

Segelinde sighed with relief.

"Come", she said, and took me into the hall where Cai was teaching Adelgunde to read.

I inclined my head to greet Cai and he said: "Only back now? Took longer than I thought."

My wife looked at Adelgunde and said: "They are back. I saw them all, over by their hall."

Adelgunde smiled and left the hall with Aritê in tow while my wife handed me a horn of ale.

I raised my eyebrows in surprise. "So, what was that all about?"

Adelgunde had become close to my family, not unlike an adopted daughter.

She scowled and shook her head. "Men are truly blind. Have you not noticed that Adelgunde has an interest in Hostilius? Have you not seen how she looks at him?"

My jaw dropped and I stared at her blankly. "Hostilius?" I responded with a slight smile.

"He is a hard man", I said. "A killer. One of the meanest bastards I know. And Adelgunde is only… she can't be older than twenty-two summers?"

Segelinde placed her hands on her hips. Which did not bode well for me.

"Killer. Hard man. Bastard. Messenger of the war god. Does it sound familiar to you?"

"Yes, but… "

"But nothing! You will not interfere. They are only friends. For now, anyway. Don't ruin it for them before it starts. Hostilius is a gentle, kind-hearted man."

To hear the name of my friend associated with words like 'kind' and 'gentle' almost caused me to choke on the ale and burst out laughing. Applying more than a little self-restraint, I managed to avert my exile from our hall.

"Of course I will not interfere. Whatever makes them happy."

She narrowed her eyes and issued a muted high pitched yelp. "Go outside, Eochar. You are infested with lice and fleas!"

She added as an afterthought: "And don't go near Aritê or Little Nik. You will infect them too."

I complied. It was Cai who came to the rescue.

"Aritê go with Egnatius to pick pretty flowers. We grow them on farm back in Sirmium. I plant seeds when we arrive."

I scowled. "I don't need to smell nice, Cai. I need to get rid of the lice."

"You help me, Lucius of the Da Qin. No complain, just help."

Later I watched with interest as he crushed the heap of flowers to a pulp in a wooden bowl. He sent a servant to prepare a bath and added half the flower paste to the hot water. "Why only half?" I queried.

He held out the remaining half. "This for centurion Hostilius", he said.

He held up a flower by the stem. It was pure white, with a golden centre. "Greeks call this 'golden flower'. Bathe now. You see."

I bathed for at least half a watch, dunking my head under the water many times while holding my breath.

When I finally left the bath, I could see dead lice on the surface of the water.

I donned a clean tunic and Cai announced my arrival at the hall. "Husband clean. I go deal with kind-hearted Primus Pilus now."

Chapter 8 – Oathbreaker (January 245 AD)

The cold of winter did not stop the blossoming affection between the Primus Pilus and Adelgunde. As instructed, I did not interfere. That is, until I was asked to.

Hostilius and I were out hunting, on his insistence. I could see that he wanted to tell me something, but that he had difficulty putting it into words.

Eventually, after riding in silence for long, he said out of the blue: "Adelgunde really is a nice girl, Lucius."

"Yes, Primus Pilus, I agree. She is like a daughter to me."

I must have said the wrong thing, for my words were followed by another extended period of silence.

I realised over time that Segelinde had been right. When it came to women, Hostilius was kind and soft-spoken, but in male company he was quick to anger.

"For Jupiter's sake, Domitius, don't act like you're a bloody fool!"

I grinned. Just like a fool would.

"Adelgunde and I will be getting married", he said. "And you are going to help me make it happen."

"Of course, Primus Pilus, I will have it no other way", I replied. "Why didn't you just say so from the start?"

"Because you've known all along and you didn't encourage me", he said. "I thought that you disapproved."

I waved it away and took ownership of my wife's advice. "I just didn't wish to interfere."

His whole demeanour softened. "There really is a gentle side to you, Domitius. I would never have thought that a hard-arsed killer like you can be compassionate."

In any event, an ecstatic Segelinde suggested that we play the role of Adelgunde's parents since she was an orphan for all practical purposes.

During the month that followed, our house was abuzz with women seeing to arrangements. I developed a sudden affinity for hunting, leaving the women to their quest.

On one of these excursions I was accompanied by Marcus, Vibius, as well as a somewhat nervous Hostilius.

"How come you seem nervous, Centurion?" Marcus asked. "I have seen you standing in the front rank with thousands of Sasanian heavy cavalry charging. You appeared less flustered then."

Hostilius scowled. "It is cheap words for a man not yet bound to a woman."

He was looking for allies. "Tell him, Domitius", Hostilius added.

I grinned. "True words, Primus Pilus. I would rather charge the Hun horde than face my wife when she is angry."

Segelinde had explained to me what would be required in terms of the wedding ceremony.

I half-turned in the saddle to face Hostilius. "In this part of the world, the husband is expected to present a dowry to the wife", I said.

"I assume you mean jewellery, dresses and coin. The stuff women would want, eh?" he asked, with a desperate look about him.

"No Primus Pilus, not at all. The dowry is supposed to consist of horses and oxen. The horses are to be fully kitted out with saddles and the necessary tack. In addition, a proper shield, javelin and sword need to accompany the animals."

I could see his face brighten. "I'll be damned."

I held up my hand. "Before you get too excited, Primus Pilus, remember your dowry is required to fit the station of the girl and be acceptable to her family. I am lenient, but knowing my wife, I think this is not going to come cheap. The good news is that the wife needs to present weapons to her husband. It is a gesture to show that the woman will support her husband and fight at his side when necessary."

He grinned then. "The Romans have a lot to learn from the Goths."

The moon preceding the wedding passed quickly.

Although we had buried most of our coin on the farm in Sirmium, we brought along enough to still be considered extremely wealthy. Hostilius presented his wife to be with a dowry worthy of a princess. In my role as the father of the bride, I got to choose the weapons and Hostilius received a magnificent Scythian bow as well as a pattern-welded short sword that cost me a goodsome share of my fortune.

We built another hall on the property which Hostilius and his new wife would occupy.

* * *

In later years I heard a wise man describe peace as the short time spans that separated long periods of conflict. I was about to find out that it was fast becoming the norm in our lives.

I rarely socialised with Kniva as he was a hands-on king who did not rest on his laurels. When I was summoned to attend him, I knew that there was trouble afoot.

He dismissed his servants and guards on my arrival after I had been handed the customary horn of ale.

"Brother, I have received disturbing news. My delegation, tasked to collect the annual tribute from the Empire, returned empty-handed. The emperor's message said that the Goths, Roxolani and Carpiani had deserted during the campaign against the Sasanians, therefore we had broken our oaths. I have received word, the Greuthungi are in a similar position."

He stood, agitated. "By all the gods, Eochar, we bled for Rome. Now the Arab is calling us oathbrakers. My minor lords count on the funds. Soon they will be baying for blood. Roman blood. I do not know whether I will be able to stop them."

He drank a swig from his horn. "You know, brother, I do not think I would want to stop them."

I approached him and placed my hand on his shoulder. "Your enemy is my enemy, no matter who they are."

"As long as your enemy is not the Roxolani", I added. "My wife is the daughter of their king, you know."

*　*　*

It did not take long for the resentment to build north of the Danube. The tribes were angry, cheated out of their tribute.

Within days we received a message from Ostrogotha the Patient. It sounded all but patient: an invitation to attend a council of war. Similar requests went to the Carpiani and the Roxolani. The emperor's oathbreaking was uniting the tribes, providing them with a common enemy.

Chapter 9 – Reunion

Half a moon had passed before we received news of the imminent arrival of King Bradakos of the Roxolani.

Many moons before, I travelled through the lands of the Roxolani in the company of Kniva. There the unthinkable happened when Bradakos, king of the fearsome Royal Scythians, provided hospitality to the iudex of the mighty Thervingi.

I was part of the small retinue that accompanied the iudex to the borderlands of the Thervingi to await the arrival of my friend and mentor.

On the second day a messenger announced the arrival of the king. I forded the river and rode out to meet them.

Bradakos was escorted by a retinue of twenty warriors, which included Elmanos and Gordas. They formed the vanguard, riding half a mile ahead, accompanied by two of the king's underlings.

Gordas clasped my arm and shook his head. "When I am close to you, I can feel it in my bones. I can sense the gathering of the clouds of war, Eochar. You truly are the war god's servant", he said, grinning from ear to ear.

I slapped the Hun on the shoulder. "It is good to see you too, Gordas. By the way, my daughter sends her love."

Interestingly, Gordas viewed Aritê not as a child but as a princess, albeit a smaller version. He was visibly moved and suddenly turned serious. "Tell the princess that Gordas of the Huns is forever her servant."

I knew better than to make fun of his statement. "I will do as you ask."

With the Huns at my side, I rode to greet my friend.

Passing the reins to a Hun warrior, I dismounted at a respectful distance.

The king sat atop a magnificent straw-coloured stallion with a black mane, dwarfing my Hun horse, Simsek.

Bradakos's armour was of excellent quality, devoid of decorations or anything of an ornate nature. The King must have seen forty summers, yet it was clear that he was formidable. Once he had been the champion of the Roxolani. Bulging muscles were clearly visible where the thick scale armour did not conceal it. This was not a man who had succumbed to the temptations of an easy life. He was a warrior to the core.

I went down on one knee and inclined my head in respect.

"Rise, Prince Eochar of the Roxolani", he said, smoothly dismounting as only a Scythian can. He clasped my arm. As always, I was amazed by the subtle message of power conveyed by his grip. Although he did not squeeze my arm, his grip was made of iron.

Then he embraced me, sending a clear message to his underlings that I was a man who carried his favour.

"I can feel in your grip that you have not grown soft", he said and slapped my shoulder.

With Gordas forming the vanguard, I rode in the company of the king, his noblemen following behind, allowing us to converse in private.

"I see that you could not resist bringing Gordas along", I said.

"It is ever a good thing to remind the Goths to whom we are allied to, just in case they start getting ideas above their station", he replied.

"Kniva the Goth has given me much, but in here", I hit my chest with my fist, "I am still a Roxolani."

Bradakos grunted his approval.

"Will you fight against Rome?" he asked.

I explained how it came to be that I gave a pledge to Ostrogotha the Patient. I told Bradakos how events have played out thereafter.

"The Venedi and the Fenni are lethal within the confines of the forests and swamps. You did well to draw them into the open", he said, fascinated by my tale.

Despite his rough demeanour, he was a thinker. "Would you fight against me, against your own people, if the Greuthungi king demands it of you?"

I couldn't help but smile, as his words reflected thoughts I had wrestled with.

For a second time that day I placed my hand on my chest and grinned. "I am a Scythian in there", then I tapped my finger against my temple, "but, I am a Roman up here."

He nodded and returned my grin, understanding the unspoken words.

"Now, let us ride with haste", he said, "I cannot wait to see my granddaughter."

We made our way back to the Thervingi stronghold, finding that the Carpiani had arrived during our absence.

I became acquainted with their king, Tarbus, three years earlier under less than ideal circumstances. The IV Italica, the legion we were affiliated to, entrapped a large warband of the

Carpiani using scarce white Spanish horses as bait. I subsequently visited with the king, accompanied by my Carpiani friend, Thiaper, to negotiate a foedus agreement between the barbarians and Rome.

While the kings greeted I kept a respectful distance. To my surprise, Tarbus motioned for me to join them. I approached, then went down on one knee and inclined my head.

"You did not afford me the same level of respect last time we met, Prince Eochar?" he asked with an amused expression adorning his scarred face.

"A Roman officer kneels only to his emperor", I replied.

"So what are you these days? If not a Roman, are you a Scythian? A Goth maybe?" He smiled a mocking smile.

I had pondered on the same question for many moons so I was ready with an answer. I rose, not willing to play the humble underling for long. "My only allegiance is to Arash, the god of war and fire."

I delivered the words with a measured chill and I could see that it had unsettled him. He knew I was among friends, men who owed me their lives many times over. Men who would not lift a hand against me if I challenged him.

A sudden, uncomfortable silence descended. Tarbus's eyes darted from left to right and he smiled a thin smile. "It is good to see you, Prince Eochar."

"Thank you, Lord Tarbus", I replied. I walked away.

I arranged for Bradakos and his retinue to stay over at my home. The Carpiani have been allied to the Thervingi for years so we left Kniva and Tarbus to continue their discussions in private. We would feast together on our return from the Greuthungi.

"What was that all about?" Bradakos asked when we were out of earshot.

I sighed. "Bradakos, since my father was murdered, it feels as if something inside me has died with him. I will show respect where it is due, but I will not tolerate a man the likes of Tarbus to humiliate me. As a prince of the Scythians, I was within my rights to challenge him."

My mentor grinned. "I have never been too fond of Tarbus. He is inclined to pettiness." My friend chuckled. "He almost wet his pants when you rose and spoke of Arash."

"You may not realise it Eochar, but you truly have the gift to put the fear of the gods into people. They say that they see a glimpse of the wrath of Arash. Even Gordas has told me this. Not many men frighten Gordas."

I waved it away. "You imagine it, I am a reasonable man", was my honest reply.

"You know they call you 'Eochar the Merciless'?" he added.

I scowled.

The arrival of the Roxolani delegation at my house had a festive feel about it.

Segelinde had prepared for days. Even the normally dour Hostilius was drawn into the arrangements by Adelgunde.

Aritê could barely contain her excitement at the arrival of the Roxolani. My daughter immediately ran to her eternal servant, Gordas, hugging him as he dismounted. Then she approached Bradakos, holding out her arms so he could lift her onto the horse.

"Your horse is much bigger than Papa's horse, Grandpa Brakos. Is it because you are a king?"

Bradakos was fond of the little girl. "I have a larger horse so I can ride with Princess Aritê", he explained, making a vital error.

Although he clearly had the gift, he did not yet have experience with children. "So let's go for a ride now", she yelled excitedly.

It ended up with Grandpa Brakos riding around the compound at least five times before Aritê became bored with the activity.

That night we feasted.

It was unlike the normal drunken celebrations of the barbarians. To me, the feast had all the elements of a family reunion, only without the conflict.

That evening when we entered the hall, we were all equals. There were no kings, no tribunes and no princes, only friends enjoying each other's company.

We were a close-knit group who had all shared hardship over time. Bradakos, Gordas, Elmanos, Cai, Hostilius, Marcus, Vibius, Felix and even Pezhman joined us around the table. Adelgunde still felt out of place and volunteered to look after Aritê. We missed Kniva's presence, as he was also one of our inner circle, but he had to attend to his duties by entertaining the Carpiani delegation.

When all were seated, I noticed an open place set with a plate as well as a mug filled with red wine. I tried to figure out who was yet to arrive. Segelinde stood then, which would have been a major breach of etiquette in a Roman family. Yet, among the Scythians where women are the equal of men, it was normal.

"There is one who is not with us tonight. He is the one who gave his life so that I may live. He is the one who traded his life for the life of Aritê. Tonight he is feasting in the Warrior Hall of Teiwaz, with the heroes of old."

Felix rose. "He saved me as well, he did." The old soldier raised his cup above his head, "this is for you, Nik, the last of the great Romans", and finished his wine in one long swallow.

We all followed suit, then I emptied Nik's cup in the fire as an offering to Arash.

By then I was nearly unable to speak. To my surprise, Bradakos and Hostilius's eyes were also moist, which made me feel less embarrassed.

I cleared the emotion from my throat with a deep swallow of red. "I will never forget my father's sacrifice, nor will I forget the evil men who did him harm. I will have my vengeance. When? It is for Arash to decide."

From the corner of my eye I could not help but notice the approving nods of Bradakos, Gordas and Hostilius. These men were not plagued by the weakness of a forgiving nature.

Despite the sombre start to the evening, we were soon laughing, drinking and retelling the tales of our shared adventures.

We drank an acceptable red with a deep purple colour, which according to Segelinde, had "found its way" into the cellar of her brother. No doubt, spoils from a raid into Roman lands.

Servants brought wooden trays stacked with boar, deer and wild fowl, all grilled over open flames. Hostilius soon made it known that he was the sole "sponsor" of the meat, having taken a liking to hunting.

He nudged me with his elbow. "You know, Domitius, hunting boar is not that different from standing in the front ranks. You don't have a shield, but you still get to kill the pig." He continued to laugh loudly at his own attempt at humour. The Primus Pilus was no doubt gruff, but I have come to accept and love his rough and ready way.

It dawned on me then that those around the table were my real family. People for whom I would sacrifice my life if it were required. I did not doubt that they would do the same for me.

I slept fitfully that night, plagued by dreams filled with violence and angst, my visions obscured by the murk of the netherworld. Waking in a cold sweat, I could not remember the dreams nor interpret their meaning. When I look back at how events unfolded, I tell myself that I should have known better and realised that Arash had sent me a warning.

We departed early the next morning. Too early for men who feasted and drank late into the night.

78

Cai and Vibius remained behind, but Marcus, Hostilius and I joined Kniva's delegation.

Hostilius rode with Gordas, having an animated argument over which was the better weapon to hunt boar with. Spear or arrow.

Many thoughts occupied my mind and I reined in to afford myself some time to think.

Marcus soon fell in next to me. "You know Lucius, I always imagined that the barbarians attacked the lands of Rome on a whim. I now realise how wrong I was. This chieftain, Ostrogotha, seems like a clever one."

"He is very clever, Marcus. And he is a warrior, a hard bastard. Believe you me, he will have a plan, probably a good one. The challenge faced by these chieftain kings is to get other barbarian leaders to obey their commands. In this case Kniva, his son-in-law, is in his debt. The Carpiani king is, for all practical purposes, a vassal of the Thervingi and Greuthungi."

"So why did he deem it necessary to get you to pledge your assistance?" he asked.

"He knows that I have some influence over the Roxolani. Ostrogotha has no doubt heard of my reputation as a messenger of Arash and Teiwaz. Should I fight at his side, the morale of the warriors will be high."

"Disregarding the commands of a chieftain of another tribe is one thing", I added, "but to make light of the will of the god of war and fire? Well… that is another thing altogether, eh?"

"So does Mars, or Arash as you call him, really speak to you?" Marcus asked.

I was saved from answering by an almighty roar of thunder emanating from the near-purple clouds moving in from the north and west.

Marcus stared at me, suddenly also a believer. "Did he speak to you now? In the thunder?"

"Yes, he is telling me it is going to rain", I said with a serious expression.

Marcus scowled. The scowl disappeared in an instant and he held up both hands, palms open towards me, sensing my reluctance to discuss the subject. "I understand Lucius, and I apologize. What happens between you and the god is none of my business."

Hostilius and Gordas approached at a trot, then fell in beside us.

The Primus Pilus proudly produced a hooded cloak from his saddlebag. "This is made from the pelt of a seal. One can ride with this in the rain all day, yet never feel the damp on your skin."

Gordas inspected the leather, clearly impressed. "What is a seal?" he asked.

"In the cold seas to the north, lives a creature that resembles a dog without legs", Hostilius explained. "Rather than legs, the gods gave it fins, like a fish."

Gordas was clearly not convinced. "A trading man once tried to sell me armour made from the skin of a dragon." He pointed to a scalp, one of many adorning his saddle, and smiled his wolflike smile.

Hostilius scowled while draping the cloak around his armoured shoulders. He looked less sure of himself, yet still rebuffed the Hun. "It is no tall tale, Gordas."

The Hun snorted indignantly and pulled his furs tighter as the first large raindrops fell. Then the heavens opened.

Chapter 10 – The Crow (March 245 AD)

The storm raged around us. Purple-black clouds made it seem as if evening had descended, although it was not yet noon. The heavy rain made it difficult to see more than twenty paces ahead.

There was no shelter to be had, leaving us with no option but to keep our heads down and ride on.

Veins of lightning illuminated the sky and the dirt track soon resembled a small stream. We were forced to travel parallel to the road to lessen the chances of the horses slipping in the mud.

Within a watch the violent spring storm passed, leaving us all soaked to the bone. Except Hostilius, of course, whose clothes were drier than a camel's arse. To his credit, he did not harp on the fact, but his half-smirk clearly said 'I told you so'.

The gods were kind enough to favour us with summery weather for the remainder of the journey.

In the early afternoon on the fifth day after leaving the Thervingi settlement, we were fifteen miles from the stronghold of Ostrogotha, king of the Greuthungi Goths.

Gordas rode at my side. Without turning his head he said in a low voice: "Men have been watching us from the hills for a while." He sniffed the air. "They smell like Goths."

I was not convinced that he was blessed with such an acute sense of smell, but I nodded as I had also become aware of the activity.

"Be ready, Gordas, but I am sure that they are the scouts of King Ostrogotha", I speculated.

For a change, it turned out that I was right. We travelled another ten miles in the direction of the Greuthungi settlement when we noticed the dust stirred up by a small band of approaching horsemen.

Anticipating the arrival of the Greuthungi king, his peers, Kniva, Bradakos and Tarbus, rode to the front of our delegation.

Ostrogotha led the group of horsemen, which I assumed to be his oathsworn.

His mount immediately drew my attention, a magnificent pure black stallion. Not as large as the Roxolani horses, but still an impressive specimen. Like Bradakos, his armour and weapons were workman-like. He wore no helmet, an indication of peaceful intent.

Both parties came to a halt when they were twenty paces apart. Ostrogotha was the first to act, dismounting gracefully, followed by his hearth warriors. The visiting kings dismounted heartbeats later, as did the rest of us. It was considered an insult to be in an elevated position in relation to the king.

He walked up to Kniva, embraced him, and spoke loudly for all to hear. "Welcome, son. It gladdens me to see you well." He briefly clasped arms with Tarbus, the vassal king, then he turned to face Bradakos.

Bradakos was half a head taller than Ostrogotha, but not quite as broad in the shoulders.

The Greuthungi king extended his arm and Bradakos clasped it in a sign of friendship. "Your reputation precedes you, King Bradakos of the Roxolani. Welcome to the lands of the Greuthungi."

Bradakos nodded, acknowledging his words.

The Goth's gaze drifted over our entourage and lingered on me for half a heartbeat. He inclined his head, ever so slightly, in recognition of my presence. I imagined a smile touching the corners of his mouth.

He spoke to the kings. "Let us not remain here with parched throats. Come, join me in my hall."

The entourages followed forty paces behind, affording the kings an opportunity to converse in private.

The hillfort of the Greuthungi was close by and soon we walked our horses through the natural gap which provided the only access to the summit of the hill. The top of the hill was flat, surrounded by rocky cliffs inaccessible to horsemen. In times of danger, the townsfolk and warriors living in the sprawling settlement would seek refuge within the natural fortifications. They would bring enough food and livestock to endure a short siege. Ample water was available from a spring on the summit. The enemies of the Greuthungi were the horse warriors of the Sea of Grass. Not the type of men who possessed the patience for a protracted siege.

I took time, as was my habit, to study the defences. I tried to identify weaknesses and thought on how I would attack this position, as well as the manner in which I would defend it.

Before he entered the hall, Bradakos walked over to me.

"The kings will now gather in the hall of Ostrogotha. We have suggested that, as is the custom, we will all be accompanied by the war leader of the tribe. I have asked Elmanos to join me." I felt relieved that I would not have to partake, but slightly insulted as well, for obvious reasons.

"We all agreed that there is no doubt that Arash speaks through you", Bradakos said. "When you take the field, all know the outcome of the battle. Kniva shared with us what you had done in the lands of the Sasanians." He lowered his voice. "Although Tarbus has not acknowledged it, Thiaper has told me how you had humiliated the Carpiani. Ostrogotha specifically asked that you join us." He thought for a moment, then added: "If he had not, either Kniva or I would have insisted."

I realised that Tarbus was still disgruntled as a result of my actions years earlier. What I did not realise then was that he resented me. Nor did I know how strong the feelings were.

Before long, we all gathered in the hall. Apart from Ostrogotha, each king was accompanied by a noble of importance.

Servants appeared and laid down wooden platters heavy with beef, mutton and deer.

Slaves handed us horns brimming with golden ale. They did not leave the hall, but stood at the ready, in case any needed a refill. Bradakos gave the slaves an enquiring glance.

"We may speak freely today, Lord Bradakos", Ostrogotha said, and gestured for a slave to come forward. He approached, ready to refill the king's horn, but the big Goth waved it away.

"Open your mouth, slave." The man complied and I could see that his tongue had been crudely removed.

The Greuthungi grinned. "He will not pass on what he hears today." He gestured towards the others. "Rather safe than sorry, eh?"

Before he could continue, a warrior, tall and broad, was ushered into the hall. Ostrogotha nodded to his bodyguards, accepting the presence of the new arrival.

"I have come as you have requested, lord", the man said, inclining his head.

From the dust and mud on his clothes, it was obvious that he had travelled far. He wore thick scale armour extending to his knees. At his side hung a longsword, the pommel wrapped with leather. Black boiled leather vambraces protected his forearms and grey iron greaves his lower legs. I noticed the battle lines criss-crossing the armour and the scars on his exposed skin. Some still red and angry, others old and white.

He removed his full-face helmet, hung with thick chain to protect his bull-like neck.

His hair was black and fell loose about his shoulders, still wet from the exertion of the ride. Unlike his hair, his eyes were light grey, almost white.

Surprisingly he was clean-shaven, revealing a red, welted scar that ran from above his right eye all the way down to the corner of his mouth. The rest of his face was ordinary, maybe even handsome, but strangely expressionless. Not unlike that of a corpse staring with eyes devoid of life.

"Welcome, lord Cannabaudes." Ostrogotha gestured for the warrior to take a seat next to him.

"Cannabaudes is Erilaz, war leader", Ostrogotha explained. "He is the one who leads the campaign against the terrible Alani horde in the eastern lands of the Greuthungi. We call him by his warrior name, 'The Crow'."

Again I was tempted to assume that the origin of his name had to do with his raven black hair, but by now I knew better.

Cannabaudes inclined his head to each of the kings as they were introduced. When it was my turn, Ostrogotha said: "This is Eochar, Prince of the Roxolani."

The Crow clasped my arm with a grip intended to intimidate. He looked at me with his emotionless corpse-eyes. "I have heard your name, Roxolani", he growled.

As he took my arm, I experienced a strange sensation that I was unable to place. Looking back, the only explanation I can find is that I somehow sensed evil lurking within him.

Wrong-footed, I was only able to nod. He held my gaze for a while longer then retired to sit at the right hand side of the king.

Ostrogotha drank from his horn. "For many years we have spilled our blood for Rome, protecting the borders against its enemies. We have kept our warriors on a tight leash, with very few incursions into their lands. The boy emperor was true to his word, but this man, this usurper from the east, the one they call 'the Arab', is an oathbreaker." He spat on the floor. "He is a nithing."

He looked me in the eye. "You have met this man, Prince Eochar?"

"I have, he is the one who murdered my father", I replied. "His word is worthless, he has no honour."

Ostrogotha knew how to rouse the emotions of men. He pointed his hand at me. "Even his own warlord, the commander of the iron legions, has been betrayed by him."

He stood and drew his magnificent longsword. "This is the only thing that the Arab will understand. He needs to feel the wrath of the warriors of the Sea of Grass."

"I would hear your thoughts", he said, rammed his sword into the wooden floor next to him, and sat down. A tongueless slave immediately rushed over and filled his empty horn to the brim.

Bradakos spoke then. "The Empire is a good ally and a bad enemy. We have lived in peace with them ever since I can remember, but we cannot allow them to break the agreement and remain unpunished. There has to be consequences."

He drank and continued: "Rome is withdrawing legions from Dacia. The border fortifications are weak. The oathbreaker can no longer rely on the protection of the Roxolani. I say we breach the limes on the Dacian border. From there we can either raid the land beyond the forest, or we could cross the Danube and strike deep into Moesia. It will be good if the Carpiani would join us. We will travel on horseback, to strike swiftly, then retreat. It would be foolish to get involved in a pitched battle with the legions on ground that favours them."

Tarbus nodded. "I have heard that the limes that run from north to south on the eastern border of Dacia, close to the Alutus River, is weakly garrisoned. Small groups of my young warriors breach it regularly. Once we have crossed into Dacia, we will be unopposed. Maybe we could even raid the Roman gold mines. I have heard that they store mountains of gold close to the mines."

Ostrogotha grinned. "While the Roxolani and the Carpiani ravage Dacia or Moesia, the Thervingi and the Greuthungi will join, cross the Danube, and raid deep into Moesia."

Kniva nodded. "It is a simple plan. I like it."

Ostrogotha looked at Cannabaudes. "What say you, Crow?"

"I say that the plan is good, but we should engage the Romans legions. They have grown weak. We should give battle and destroy them. Running from the legions is the act of a coward."

He glanced at Bradakos, but did not dare to call the Roxolani king a coward.

I could see the anger rise within my friend Bradakos as he clenched and unclenched his jaw muscles.

Ostrogotha intervened just in time.

"Prince Eochar?" he asked.

"The plan is good", I answered. "We must be sure to co-ordinate our attacks, but we must not engage them. Only a fool will engage the Roman legions on ground that suits infantry." I stared directly at Cannabaudes, daring him to gainsay me. I found that as I grew older, my capacity for suffering fools diminished greatly.

The Crow stood, his hand on the hilt of his sword. "Watch your tongue, Roman."

I glanced across at Kniva, who shook his head almost imperceptibly. It took every ounce of self-restraint not to respond to the challenge. I remained seated.

Cannabaudes smirked, saying softly as if to himself, yet loud enough for some to hear: "I thought not."

He had crossed the line and I could feel the rage of Arash building within as my hand went to my sword. Then Ostrogotha stood.

"Let us toast our good fortune. It is not often that the Goths and the Horse People join a common cause. We will teach Rome a lesson and become rich with loot."

All stood and drank deeply from their horns. I could feel the rage, still present, but abating.

Kniva walked towards me and placed his hand on my shoulder. He whispered then: "Thank you, brother. I do not know whether I could have done what you just did."

"Let us feast now, to celebrate our plans. We will talk about the details when we become sober", Ostrogotha said, smiling warmly. His guards summoned the rest of our delegation inside and soon we were joined by the nobles of the Greuthungi.

My eyes searched for The Crow, but I could not find him among the milling warriors in the hall. Ostrogotha walked up to me. Gone was the friendly diplomatic façade. He now wore a mask of iron. "Cannabaudes is getting ideas above his station", he growled. "I have sent him away to do penance. He will return to the frontier in the east."

Chapter 11 – Oath

With Cannabaudes's macabre presence removed, the feast turned into an enjoyable affair.

There was something that intrigued me so I decided to exact an explanation from my brother-in-law.

"Kniva, I am sure that you have told me that your formal name is also Cannabaudes. Is the Crow another member of your extended family? Like your cousin Werinbert?"

A couple of years earlier I had assisted Kniva to resolve a family tiff. His cousin Werinbert had tried to usurp the throne and ended up a corpse.

Kniva scowled. "Cannabaudes is a special name among my people. It is only given to the eldest son of those descended from the old gods, the Aesir. Those who carry the sacred name are the ones eligible to wear the crown."

He drank from his horn and continued. "The Crow yields significant power among the Greuthungi. He is cunning and brutal. The warriors follow him because he wins wars and he gives much gold. Be careful, Eochar, he will not forget."

I did not say it, but neither would I.

The Greuthungi king was an excellent host. The ale flowed freely into the night and the platters of freshly grilled meat were replaced even before they were empty.

On the insistence of Ostrogotha, Kniva relayed the tale of my fight with Hygelac the White, war leader of the Heruli. Afterwards, my brother-in-law produced the famous sword of Teiwaz, "Oathbringer". All the Greuthungi insisted on touching the ancient weapon, inscribed with the magic runes of the old gods. To a man, they swore that the power of the Aesir was palpable in the blade.

I realised then the cunning of Ostrogotha. When I fought as Kniva's champion and defeated the giant Heruli, Kniva's position among the Greuthungi was elevated. In turn, this increased Ostrogotha's status in the eyes of his nobles through his association with Kniva by marriage.

Yet, I noticed something no one else did. There was a glint in Kniva's eye as he held the hilt of "Oathbringer" when the nobles touched the blade. I could not help but smile inwardly. The brother of my wife harboured greater ambitions.

Later on during the evening, slaves stacked heaps of soft furs against the log walls of the hall, allowing the guests to take what they required and settle in for the night. Slowly the sounds of conversation and raucous laughter were replaced by loud snoring, interspersed with an occasional grunt.

I slept fitfully as I was never one who enjoyed the Gothic way of communality.

As is always the case with consuming excess quantities of ale, the warriors started stirring a full watch before sunrise to answer nature's call.

As I woke, I sensed an approaching shape in the dark. Before I had gathered my wits, I felt a stabbing pain in my left foot.

"Bloody fat Goth", Hostilius mouthed in Latin, stumbling in the dark towards the doorway.

Ever since the Primus Pilus fought shoulder to shoulder with Bradakos against the Vandali, they shared the bond of the warrior.

Hostilius must have passed out close to the Roxolani, as he and Bradakos earlier picked up where they left off, reliving the fight while plying one another with ale.

In the field adjacent to the hall, servants were grilling smoked joints of pork over open fires.

The bulk of the guests moved outside, leaving only the council of kings and their war leaders. I was pleased to notice that Guntharic, rather than Cannabaudes, sat on the right of Ostrogotha.

"The Thervingi and Greuthungi will cross the river at the next full moon, twenty-eight days from today. One moon later, the

Carpiani and Roxolani will breach the limes and enter Dacia. We will win loot, which is our rightful payment in terms of the agreement with the Arab. Once our purses bulge with gold, we will retreat."

His gaze met mine. "The messenger of Arash is wise. We will not engage with the iron legions where they are strong. We will mock them and return home rich."

He swallowed down a piece of pork with ale. "But, the day will come when Rome will taste our iron. That day is not far away."

The barbarian kings cheered his words. All were in agreement.

He held up his hand. "And... we will not make war on each other while we are dealing with the Empire."

And then the kings, all great men of honour, sealed their agreement with the sacred oath of the Sea of Grass.

Once they had concluded the ritual of the blood oath, we all prepared to take the road home.

On that morning, something unbeknown to us took place in the hall of Ostrogotha the Patient. A shift occurred. Not earth-shattering, not even worth retelling at the time. But happen, it did. And it is undeniable.

In the lands north of the Danube, all still went about their business. The warriors trained at their craft, the boys tended the herds and the children played amongst the shelters.

A thousand miles to the west, in the greatest city on earth, Phillip the Arab was cementing his position as emperor. He had taken the decision earlier to break his foedus agreement with the wild tribes. Probably he had thought it a move of no consequence.

But yet, that unremarkable decision led us to the hall of Ostrogotha.

In time, the consequences would change the face of the world.

Chapter 12 – Invasion (May 245 AD)

(A crude map of Roman Dacia is available on my website www.hectormillerbooks.com)

Kniva and his father-in-law led the Gothic coalition that crossed the Danube far to the east, ravaging Moesia Inferior and raiding even as far south as Thracia.

The Scythian army was camped fifteen miles to the east of the Dacian limes, which lay some miles east of the Alutus, and north of the Danube.

It would be more accurate to say that there were two armies. The Roxolani, led by Bradakos, and the Carpiani, commanded by Tarbus.

The two tribes rarely clashed, but it soon became apparent that Bradakos and Tarbus's views on things martial were not just different. They were irreconcilable in most cases.

Were it not for the presence of Thiaper, my friend and second in command of the Carpiani, the situation would have been unbearable.

The weather resembled that of summer, rather than late spring. We sat on comfortable furs outside Bradakos's spacious tent. Five paces away two sheep were roasting over a roaring fire, tended by a young oathsworn. The fat and juices hissed as it dripped onto the smoking embers.

No other tents were pitched closer than forty paces, allowing us the privacy to converse freely. The king's guards assured that none strayed close, by accident or intentionally.

Hostilius was using his ancient Gothic dagger to slowly carve up a piece of dried, salted deer meat.

My Persian scout cum Saka warrior, Pezhman, joined us for the evening. He regarded it as a great honour to be dining in the company of a king and sat wide-eyed, listening to the conversation.

I could see he was itching to ask a question, but unsure whether he was allowed to.

"Pezhman, what troubles you?" I asked. "Tonight we are not kings, princes or tribunes. We are all friends enjoying each other's company."

"Lord, I do not understand why Rome is here, on this side of the Great River?"

"Pezhman, I will try to explain."

"Imagine the Danube as a straight line, running from Sirmium in the west, to the Dark Sea in the east. A natural boundary gifted to Rome by the gods. That is, until Emperor Traianus conquered the Dacian tribes a hundred and fifty years ago.

Since then, Dacia sits like an out-of-place wart on the northern side of the Danube."

"To the west of Dacia live the Yazyges, to the east the Roxolani, Carpiani and Thervingi. North of Dacia, the Costoboci and Vandali are fighting for supremacy."

"Yes lord, but why did the Great Emperor Lord take Dacia?" he asked.

I took a deep swallow to wet my throat. "Rome conquered Dacia for its minerals. Gold, copper and salt are mined in huge quantities to supply the insatiable appetite of the Empire. Most of the mines are situated on a plateau in the centre of Dacia, surrounded by the Carpathian Mountains. This hilly area is called Transsilvania, only accessible via a limited number of mountain passes. It is a place of much wealth."

Pezhman was gaining momentum.

"Why is it called Transsilvania, lord?"

"It means 'the land beyond the forest'."

Bradakos appreciated Pezhman's curiosity. "We are camped on the edge of the plain. To the north, beyond these fortifications, are dense forests. To the south and west lies the Great River and eventually the Iron Gates."

"What are the 'Iron Gates' great Horse King?"

"Pezhman, the Iron Gates is the narrow pass that connects the lands of the Roxolani with the lands of the Yazyges", Bradakos explained. "It runs through the lands of the Romans, but we were given the right to traverse these lands by Emperor Marcus Aurelius, a great king of the Romans from long ago."

I could see the anger rise in Bradakos as he spoke through gritted teeth. "Now this usurper, Philip the Arab, has closed the route to our people. The Yazyges can no longer trade with the east, nor with the Roxolani. But not for long, young Pezhman. We will open this corridor or die trying."

Pezhman was intimidated by Bradakos's anger and nodded. He kept any further curiosity in check.

Bradakos brought his wooden cup to his lips and slowly sipped the rich red wine. "Tarbus is planning to storm the border fortifications on the morrow. He will simply try to overwhelm the Roman garrison with numbers. He has asked that the Roxolani join him."

He drank another swallow. "Well, maybe 'ask' is the wrong word to use. He assumes that the Roxolani will aid him."

Hostilius continued to carve up the meat, taking a back seat to the discussions, his face displaying a hint of a snarl. It was not difficult to picture him with a gladius, carving up the enemy, which was most probably what he was thinking.

Cai was the one who broke the ensuing silence. "Bad general overwhelms enemy with numbers. Good general breaks will of enemy with blade sheathed."

I must admit, it did sound appealing. None of us were overly keen to fight our former comrades. Neither did we relish the thought of storming the frontier fortifications.

Gordas was working a dark-haired scalp absentmindedly with his left hand. "Tell me about the fortifications of the Dacian limes."

"Firstly, there is a ditch, fifteen feet wide and nine feet deep", Marcus said. "Sharpened stakes are hammered into the bottom. On the far side of the ditch is a stone wall, six feet high and thirty feet wide. On top of that is a dirt rampart, topped with a wooden palisade. If you get that far, a heavily armoured legionary will skewer you with a pilum."

He wasn't done yet. "On the inside of the wall runs a Roman road so the legions can get there quickly in case of trouble. The larger forts are not integrated into the wall. They are a few hundred paces behind the wall and normally manned by auxiliaries. Mostly cavalry. The main function of the limes is to alert the legions of an intrusion, not to stop an army."

Gordas scowled. "Cai Lun of Serica, how do we break the will of the Romans?"

"Will is difficult to break", Cai replied. " Strong will stand on foundation of hope. Take away hope, then all above crumble."

I smiled then. It did not go unnoticed.

"Domitius, I know that smile. Mars has given you a plan", Hostilius said, and continued carving up the meat.

"Primus Pilus, I suggest we go hunting tomorrow. For wild boar. Afterwards, Vibius and I will break the will of the Romans."

Hostilius nodded, not looking up. "Sounds good to me."

I turned to the king. "You have the toughest task, Bradakos. You will have to restrain Tarbus from attacking the fortifications while we are hunting tomorrow."

Bradakos scowled.

I turned to Gordas. "I do need something else, Gordas. Something that probably only your warriors will be able to accomplish." The Urugundi grinned at the compliment. "Consider it done."

I refilled all of our cups, then shared my plan.

We feasted on mutton and red wine, retiring early.

The next morning I woke while it was still dark, when a stealthy hand placed a package inside my tent. Gordas had delivered on his promise. With great difficulty I fell asleep again, waking a third of a watch after sunrise.

Hostilius was pacing up and down in front of my tent, itching with anticipation. "By all the gods, Domitius, it's near afternoon. I know you have need of the rest, but really?"

He handed me a cold joint of mutton and a cup of well-watered wine. "Eat! We leave when I return with the horses."

I cut the leather cord which tightly bound the package, revealing a complete set of legionary issue clothing, compliments of Gordas. It would be better not to enquire about the fate of the unfortunate owner.

I had been a legionary for many years, fitting the clothing posed no problem. The garb was on the tight side, but ill-fitting garments were normal within the legions.

When my comrades arrived, I was looking quite the legionary, Cai having trimmed my hair and shaved my beard. Vibius, similarly attired and neatened up, sat on his horse, grinning down at me.

Hostilius handed me Simsek's reins. I mounted my horse with a jump that would have made a Hun proud. Gordas passed me a boar spear and we galloped off, in search of blood. Quite literally.

We needed blood for the ruse, and boar's blood is closest to the real thing.

Hostilius and Gordas led the hunt, while Vibius and I hung back at least a hundred paces, conversing in whispers. We rode through densely forested valleys and across shrubby hilltops with no sign of wild boar whatsoever.

After a watch of searching, we found Gordas waiting in a clearing. "We have had no luck. But do not be concerned, we will find something suitable."

I shook my head in disagreement. "The blood is better to use when the kill is fresh."

"We can use something we already have." he countered.

I narrowed my eyes. "Does this 'thing' happen to have two legs?"

"Maybe", he said, scowling. "Does it matter?"

"We will search for a boar", I said

"You truly are a strange one", he said, shaking his head. "In battle you are a killer, the equal of which I have never seen. You reap corpses as if you are the god of death himself. Yet, you do not wish for me to kill a man for his blood?" He rode off while muttering incoherently. Huns.

Before long we came across a large family of boar. Hostilius managed to spear a reasonably sized animal. We found him wearing a proud grin, cutting free his spear with a small hand axe.

Vibius and I then went about our business, at last having access to all the fresh blood and guts that we could wish for.

Chapter 13 – Limes Transalutanus

We returned to the vicinity of our camp, but we did not enter, unwilling to risk the possibility of a spy forewarning the Romans of our intentions. Cai met us three miles outside the camp, bearing watered down wine and food. We wolfed down the spitted fowl, cheese and flatbread.

"Bradakos give message", Cai said. "Roxolani and Carpiani ready to attack fort tomorrow. Will do as you ask."

I nodded. Bradakos had been able to restrain Tarbus.

Hostillius returned to the camp, accompanied by Cai.

Gordas whistled three times and four Urugundi warriors appeared from the mogshade, carrying a prone body, gagged and bound.

I took Gordas aside. "When I signal, take out your dagger and growl. But for the sake of the gods, don't draw blood."

He scowled. "If I did not know you better, I would have thought you had grown soft."

Ignoring the jibe, I approached the bound auxiliary, removed the gag, and sat down next to him. He could not have seen more than twenty summers. Like Vibius, he had the dark hair and looks common to the eastern provinces.

To his credit he did not beg for mercy, neither did he insult me.

"Answer my questions soldier", I said in perfect Latin, clearly surprising him, "and you will be free to go." I glanced at Gordas, who drew his dagger and advanced on the poor boy, growling. "Or I will give you to him."

He swallowed, without a doubt terrified by my Hun friend. "I... will answer", he croaked.

It did not take long to gain the knowledge we required. As promised, I would release the boy.

Gordas relayed my instructions to the Hun warriors who appeared displeased with my decision, but they had witnessed, or heard, of what I am capable of when offended. None would dare to displease the favourite of Arash and risk my wrath.

Gordas, Vibius and I mounted, then rode south.

It took us two thirds of a watch to reach our destination, twelve miles to the south.

We hid in the shade of a clump of small shrubby trees until the sun was low in the sky. Only then did we venture forth.

The vegetation was cleared for a distance of two hundred paces on the eastern side of the Limes Transalutanus, leaving little cover for hostile barbarians such as us. We hobbled the horses close by and lay side by side on our stomachs at the edge of the cleared area, studying the fortifications.

108

The sun disappeared from view, leaving the rampart silhouetted against the fading light on the far side.

The Romans were experts at constructing and manning frontier fortifications. It is no surprise, as they had been doing it for hundreds of years.

The rampart disappeared into the landscape towards the north and south. I knew it stretched along a line of more than a hundred and forty miles. Small garrisons consisting of three contubernia of auxiliaries were housed in forts which dotted the limes, placed at intervals of a mile apart. Unsurprisingly they were referred to as milecastles. Between every two milecastles were located two watchtowers, providing the legionaries with a panoramic view as well as temporary sanctuary in case of an attack.

I could see legionaries move along the wall and in the towers, the sun reflecting off their armour and spears.

"Behind those walls is the Roman fort they call Urlueni. At any time there are at least a thousand auxiliary infantry stationed there. In addition, they probably have another sixteen turmae of auxiliary cavalry at the ready."

I pointed to a huge stone structure integrated into the wall. It was a massive multi-level fortified gatehouse with twin defensive towers. "There are gates on the inside as well as on the outside. If the gates are breached from this side, they will

109

rain death from above on anyone trying to get to the inner gates."

Gordas grunted. "We could breach the wall, but it would cost us the lives of hundreds of brave warriors."

"It will not be necessary, my friend. Before the sun sets tomorrow you will ride through those gates", I said.

Gordas grinned with anticipation. "I will look after your horses. May Arash protect you." With that he crawled away, melting into the undergrowth.

Vibius and I waited until darkness had settled in before we moved. A gusty wind blew from the east as we slowly approached the wall. Our legionary armour and weapons were carefully wrapped and tied to our backs to minimise the chance of jingling armour alerting the watchers.

We moved slowly and at my signal remained motionless for extended periods. In the dark, motion attracts attention. If a shape remains still, it is near invisible.

When we were fifty paces from the wall, we went down onto our stomachs and carefully inched closer. I touched Vibius's arm as a signal for him to stop.

Only thirty paces away, elevated above us, stood a sentry, motionless as a statue. He was silhouetted against the night sky. It was impossible to tell whether he had been alerted to our presence. For all we knew he could have been sleeping. The only thing we could do was wait.

After what seemed like an eternity, I heard the sound of footsteps approaching.

"Lucius, is everything in order?" a voice boomed. I nearly choked and had to bite my tongue at the sound of my name being called.

"All in order, centurion. Nothin' to report. Thought I noticed somethin' earlier, but you know how it is. There's always vermin or somethin' crawling out there lookin' for food, isn't it?"

"You've stood in one place for too long, that's why you're seeing things. Walk down to Fulvius and back. I will guard this section for now."

My namesake grunted something and skulked off towards the south. Above us, the shape on the wall disappeared and we heard whistling. I could hear the centurion making water over the far side of the rampart.

I pressed my mouth against Vibius's ear and whispered: "Be careful. There will be water and mud in the ditch."

We seized the opportunity presented by the distracted centurion, slowly sliding down the nine foot slope into the ditch. At the bottom, the muddy filth sloshed halfway to our knees. The smell was repulsive, to say the least. I tried not to imagine what had been discarded into the fossa.

Then disaster struck.

I stepped on what I could only guess was the decomposing carcass of a long dead animal. My right foot, which was to the front, lost all purchase, sliding forward on the slime.

I grabbed blindly and my left hand got hold of a stake, but it was too late. Momentum twisted my body and I fell backwards onto a wickedly sharp stake.

Mayhap it was Fortuna, mayhap it was Arash who intervened. It could have been both.

The chain mail in my pack, folded twice over, took the brunt of the blow. The stake imbedded into the mail, so much so that Vibius had to lift me off its point. Looking back, I was extremely fortunate. If I had fallen forwards, the stake would no doubt have pierced my chest. Without the stake breaking my fall I would have created an almighty splash which would have been noticed by the watch officer.

With more than a little assistance from the gods, we ascended the far side of the ditch unscathed, but shaken. We reached the wall without being detected, then crouched close to the stone foundation of the rampart to gather our wits.

"Lucius!" shouted the booming voice of the centurion. Again, my heart beat in my throat. I knew that he was speaking to the other guard, but still, the mention of one's name causes an involuntary reaction.

"Lucius!" it came again. I jumped.

He was losing patience. "What in Hades are you up to, you lazy bloody bastard", he yelled. I heard angry footsteps disappear down the rampart.

My hand found purchase on the top edge of the stone foundation. Within heartbeats both Vibius and I stood next to the four feet high palisade.

Forty paces to the left, we heard the centurion laying into Lucius with his vine cane. "I didn't tell you to start drinking, I told you..." and so on and so forth. 'Whack, whack' went the cane, masking our sounds as we jumped onto the walkway on top of the rampart and slid down the embankment on the other side of the wall.

We were far from safe, but no one sounded the alarm as we sprinted across the road, away from prying eyes.

We jogged five hundred paces before we reached the trees. Within the forest it was pitch black. After stumbling over roots and branches repeatedly, we decided to rather rest until morning. Wrapped up in our legionary cloaks, hidden underneath dense undergrowth, we soon fell asleep.

Chapter 14 – Sons of Mars

Although we had a stressful and tiring night, we woke before dawn.

The dense canopy prevented most of the light reaching the forest floor, but it was adequate to enable us to don our armour. We slowly made our way towards the edge of the forest, crawling the last twenty paces to lessen the chance of being seen.

The day was overcast and gloomy, the wind blowing stronger than the previous evening.

I took the time to study Vibius. His hair was clotted with blood. His mail torn, his helmet dented. Specks of dried blood and dust covered his face, exposed arms, and armour.

I noticed that he was studying me in the same way, grinning.

"Lucius, you look like you have been in a terrible battle, and lost", he whispered. "Thank you, Vibius, you do too."

"Do you have the bandages and the other things?" he asked.

I patted a leather satchel at my side. "I do."

"We had better get going", I said.

It took a while to complete the final part of our disguise. We stood, took a deep breath each, and started stumbling towards the legionary fort.

Within heartbeats, ten mounted auxiliaries trotted towards us, led by a decurion.

"Halt!" boomed the decurion. We stopped in our tracks. I had my arm around Vibius, half carrying him.

The auxiliaries surrounded us, their shields uncovered, spears levelled in our direction.

"Identify yourselves", the decurion growled.

Vibius spoke in Latin with a heavy eastern accent. "Legionary Vibius Marcellinus, First Century, *Auxilliary Cohors Aurelia Antonina Hemesenorum*, reporting as ordered sir!"

Vibius looked at me sideways. "This one took a hit to the head, decurion. His brain has been addled."

The decurion nodded in understanding, being familiar with the effects of suffering a serious blow to the head.

"We have an urgent message from our prefect for your commander", Vibius continued. He doubled over with pain, then added: "It was the last command he gave."

We were escorted to the officer in charge of the auxiliary infantry. The *tribunis cohortis* was clearly a military man, an equestrian by birth. He reminded me of my friend Hostilius Proculus. My confidence dwindled upon laying eyes upon him, but Vibius was unaffected.

The officer took one look at us, then instructed the decurion: "Call for the surgeon immediately." "And", he added as an afterthought, "for the sake of the gods, give them chairs."

"While we wait for the surgeon, tell me all", he commanded.

My friend relayed our story to the scowling officer. "Our unit is stationed at the fort at Izbasesti, north of here, sir. Yesterday afternoon we were attacked by a warband of Scythians. My guess is that they are Carpiani, sir. Bloody thousands, sir. They somehow overran the watchtowers before we could be warned. Next thing, they were amongst us, sir. We tried to fight them, but there were just too many of the bastards."

By this time, the tribune had lost his scowl and studied us intently.

Before he could reply, an auxiliary entered the office, saluting smartly. "My apologies, sir. There are clouds of black smoke rising above Izbasesti in the north, sir. The fire is massive. Looks like the fort is burning." The tribune stood then, but the soldier wasn't done yet. "Same goes for the south, sir. Seems like the fort at Crampoia is going up in flames as well."

Just then a rotund officer walked through the door, sweating profusely. The tribune stood, saluted and came to attention.

My hopes soared as I identified the commanding officer of Urlueni, the *praefectus alae*. Clearly a patrician, holding military appointment in advancement of his political career.

The cavalry prefect stammered: "All the forts are on fire, tribune. There is a crisis! What are you doing about it?"

He then noticed our presence for the first time.

"Who are you?" he asked.

Vibius did not waste time. "Prefect, sir, we have escaped the destruction of Izbasesti only with the assistance of Fortuna. We hid in the Raven Forest and witnessed the cruelty of the barbarians with our own eyes. Last night we crossed back over the muddy river and walked down the valley."

The surgeon, summoned earlier, arrived just as Vibius doubled over with pain again.

"Please allow me to have a look", he said and the prefect nodded. "Just get on with it, I need him to finish his report."

The surgeon cut a piece of the bandage away and lifted the torn armour. A length of silvery grey intestine sagged from the wound. The putrid smell that accompanied it made the prefect's hand go to his mouth as he tried to hold down the bile.

The surgeon, confronted with this horrendous wound, immediately wrapped another bandage around Vibius's abdomen.

He leaned over to me, shifting the bloody bandage on my head. Splinters of bone and brain showed themselves and he jerked his hand away as if from a viper.

He stood, shaking his head imperceptibly at the prefect and tribune. "Better question them quickly", he said and left the room.

I moaned while Vibius grinded his teeth, beset by spasms.

"They cut out the eyes and tongues of all the officers" Vibius said. "Then they killed them, using their horses to pull off one limb at a time. I can still hear their screams in my head."

Another soldier entered the room. "Prefect, there are thousands upon thousands of Scythians outside the wall. They are not attacking, but moving north towards Izbasesti."

By now the plump prefect was white as a newly bleached tunic.

Vibius was not through yet. "The last thing our tribune told us before we got separated, was to get a message to Urlueni. He said to say that all was lost. They are too many too resist. He said to call for the legions. It is a full-scale invasion."

The prefect was convinced. "We will leave immediately. Our duty is to alert the legions. We will not fail Rome."

I could not help but wonder whether his first loyalty, in this case, was to himself.

Within less than a third of a watch, the garrison of Urlueni was marching west at pace.

To his credit, the patrician prefect was last to leave. As he passed us by on his magnificent gelding, he paused. "Will you be travelling with us?" he asked although he already knew the answer.

"We will make our last stand right here, sir", Vibius said and drew his gladius.

"Go with Fortuna", he said, "I salute you, you are truly sons of Mars", and spurred his horse to catch up with the infantry marching away at double pace.

When the last legionary disappeared into the distance, we removed the bandages and discarded the boar intestines. Then we washed the stinking pig blood off in the horses' drinking trough. Having neatened up, we walked the three hundred paces to the limes to open the twin gates.

The Scythian invasion had begun.

Chapter 15 – Roman feast

A smiling Gordas was the first to ride through the gates, leading Simsek. Hostilius rode alongside him, leading Vibius's mount.

We were waiting for them, greeting them as they entered.

The hulking Hun smiled broadly. "My friend, the children of our children will tell of this. For generations the name of Gordas will resound across the Sea of Grass. They will tell of Eochar the favourite of Arash, Vibius the speaker of tongues and Hostilius the hunter."

Vibius and Hostilius grinned. Praise from Gordas was rare.

"Gordas, the Roman auxiliary cavalry stationed at the nearest forts will come to investigate. We need to be ready", I interjected.

"Do not be concerned", he said. Within heartbeats the Huns split into two groups of half a thousand each. They galloped north and south respectively. The Roman auxiliaries would be annihilated.

The sun was low in the sky when the last of the Scythians rode through the gate.

Bradakos and Elmanos were close by, watching the army enter into Dacia. "We have to destroy the gates", I said.

Bradakos nodded. "See to it, Elmanos."

Elmanos inclined his head. Before long the warriors were removing the stakes from the palisade. They used the wood to build a bonfire within the gate complex which would have made the god of fire proud.

While the flames raged to the heavens we dined in style. Roman style.

Marcus, Hostilius and I sat with Bradakos and Gordas. Tarbus presented some or other excuse, while Cai insisted on meditating in private. A dead tired Vibius declined and was probably already asleep. We felt safe since the army camped all around the fort. A thousand Urugundi, five thousand Carpiani and eight thousand Roxolani.

The Roman auxiliary officers had departed in a hurry, leaving behind pantries stocked with food and cellars filled with wine.

The cook of the rotund prefect had prepared most of the dinner before the bad news arrived. Wisely he chose to depart with his master's contingent.

From the store we removed haunches of cold smoked pork. I even found a small amphora of the scarce and expensive garum made from mackerel.

On the table were bowls filled with roasted chick peas, dates, pomegranates, pears and apples.

Freshly baked white bread was heaped on a special server next to a bowl filled with wine for the purpose of dipping. It was accompanied by seeded grapes, olives and soft cheese.

On a separate platter, a variety of fruit tartlets were stacked, made with plums, pears and figs. Next to it, a bowl of honey.

We greedily swallowed down the food with gulps of excellent wine. The Roman prefect may not have been a military man, but when it came to food, he was a connoisseur.

Earlier, while Elmanos was firing the gates, Marcus and I took the opportunity to search the office of the commanding officer. He had left the office untouched when he departed in haste, as it was not a requirement for survival. There we found what we were looking for. A scroll, marked as *Itinerarium Dacia Traiana,* a detailed diagram of the roads and towns in the province. It showed distances between towns and additional detail such as 'river shallow and crossable' or 'steep, treacherous ground'. To us, it was priceless.

Before my friends became too intoxicated I unrolled the scroll and weighted it down with amphorae of wine.

Hostilius, as an ex-Primus Pilus of a legion, was familiar with an itinerary. "It is better than finding a hoard of gold."

Gordas stared at him in utter disbelief.

The Hun who, as usual, consumed wine at a faster rate than the rest of us, leaned over the table, supporting himself on his open palms pressed flat on the table. "I have seen the magic markings of the Heruli. These strange markings are similar." He swallowed another mouthful. "This is strong magic? Do you have to chant these spells during battle?"

"These markings are better than magic, Gordas", I said, "it tells me where to find loot in the land of Dacia. It shows me how many days it will take to reach towns and warns me of dangers on the road."

"Ha! I knew it. It is magic then", he said, sitting back down. "I will spread the word among the warriors that Eochar has found the Roman magic that will give us victory."

I decided to rather change the subject as soon as possible before Gordas suggested a sacrifice in order to thank the gods for their gift of magic. "Bradakos, you have done well to persuade Tarbus to relent on his idea of a frontal attack on the limes. I have never thought of you as a diplomat."

He scowled. "Why do you think Tarbus is not here tonight?"

I shrugged.

"I told him that if he goes ahead with the attack, the Roxolani and the Huns would attack him in turn", Bradakos said.

Gordas interjected. "You treated him well, king Bradakos, although it was not necessary. The Roxolani are stronger. Also, the Huns support the Roxolani."

Gordas was ever the practical type. I noticed Hostilius nodding in response to Gordas's view.

Bradakos continued, having said enough on the topic of Tarbus. "We need to move quickly. Now that we have breached the eastern limes, the legions will mobilise."

"There are two Roman legions in Transsilvania. The V Macedonica at Potaissa and the XIII Gemina at Apulum. Some cohorts might have been sent to counter the Gothic invasion in Moesia."

"How do you know?" Gordas asked.

I motioned to the scroll, still spread open on the table. "The markings told me."

He smirked, convinced he was right about the magic.

Bradakos silenced Gordas with a look. "Eochar, we need to get into Transsilvania. These lands around us are poor, but the land beyond the forest and the mountain is a rich and prosperous land."

Hostilius, Marcus and I studied the document.

"I believe it is best to head north, crossing the mountains through the Bran Pass", Hostilius said.

"It is the closest, but it is well defended by forts", Marcus added. He bent over the scroll and smiled. "They are wooden forts, though."

Bradakos was now in the lands of the Romans, an enemy he knew little of. He looked at me, a Roman, for approval, and I nodded.

"It is decided. Tomorrow we ride north", he said, and refilled his cup.

Chapter 16 – Paduroaia

On the morrow the Scythians were slow to rise. Most of the warriors had passed out the evening before, not being able to control their consumption of looted wine.

A third of a watch after sunrise the hungover army slowly took to the Roman road. Bradakos was all but satisfied. "We are in the lands of the Romans, the most feared warriors in the known world. What do we do? Drink ourselves into a stupor!"

I raised my open hand. "Peace, Bradakos. What did you expect? That they would only each have two cups, go to bed early and rise at first light?"

The king scowled, ignoring my comment. "How far to the pass that gives access to Transsilvania?"

I had studied the itinerary. "Eighty miles, if we follow the Roman road. Though there are many auxiliary forts along the way. It could take us many days to destroy them. Only a fool would leave an enemy at his back."

I watched as bands of Urugundi rode off in all directions. There would be no chance of us being surprised.

On the day the Roxolani would form the vanguard of the army. I rode alongside Bradakos and Gordas with my companions following close behind.

We had barely travelled five miles north when a Hun scout on a lathered horse galloped to report to the Hun commander.

The warrior smiled broadly. "There is no one at the fort, lord. The Romans have left everything behind that they could not carry with them. There is much loot."

The Roman fort at Izbasesti was deserted. Bradakos called a reluctant halt to allow the warriors to strip the place of anything of value left behind by the fleeing garrison. Gordas cantered away to attend to a special task I had given him.

Before long, a scowling Bradakos was issuing orders to his commanders in order to get everyone moving again. Gordas trotted up to us with seven Huns riding at his back. They escorted three clearly terrified locals.

The little party came to a halt fifty paces from us. They exchanged words and the peasants nodded their heads vigorously. Two were escorted down the column, while Gordas approached with a single villager in tow.

The Hun commander reined in beside me. "Greetings, Eochar. I have been fortunate enough to find three local men who have volunteered to be our guides."

I spotted a freshly taken scalp adorning his saddle. "And that?"

Gordas grinned. "He did not wish to volunteer."

Marcus arrived just then. "Lucius, the army will soon be advancing north, the king wishes for us to join him."

I turned to face our newly acquired guide. "Do you understand the language of the Scythians?"

"Yes, lord", he said. "Tell me about the road to the pass through the mountains which gives access to the land beyond the forests. How do we travel to get there?"

He pointed north. "We follow this Roman road, lord, while we keep the Cotmeana River on our left." His eyes kept flicking to Gordas, who wore a mildly smug expression. The guide swallowed nervously and continued. "We travel north as far as a man can walk for a day, great lord. Then at the Roman fort, the one we call Sapata, we turn north and east." Again he glanced at Gordas, who stared back at him devoid of emotion.

"Once we turn to the east, lord, it is but a single day's travel until we reach the Arges River. There is a bridge there, lord. And a great fort there lord, across the river, filled with the fierce warriors of the legions, lord."

Hostilius studied the itinerary while the scout was babbling. "It matches the directions on this", he said, and replaced the scroll in a pouch attached to his saddle.

I nodded to the guide. Gordas nodded his approval and the man visibly relaxed.

"Vibius, please escort this man to the vanguard", I said, pointing to the guide. "We will join you shortly."

I scowled at the Hun. "Gordas, stop scaring our guide. He can hardly speak. What did you tell him?"

Gordas grinned, clearly pleased with himself. "These filthy dirt-eaters are unreliable, Eochar. I merely told him that I will get a second opinion from the other two local guides. If their story differs from his, all of them will lose a finger on the first transgression, scalps on the second."

"You will do no such thing, Gordas", I said, "but I promise not to tell the guide."

Marcus rolled his eyes.

Bradakos was happy to be on the move again. "Eochar, why have the Romans withdrawn from the fort?" he asked.

The same thoughts were milling around in my mind, therefore I had an answer at the ready. "Bradakos, the limes has been built to keep barbarians from trickling across the border. More importantly for Rome, they wish to tax trade goods. Roman limites were never intended to stop a full-scale invasion, but only to delay it, to give the legions time to respond. It is of no use to them to sacrifice the garrisons."

"Also, the limites are very useful to trap an invading army once they have entered", I added.

Bradakos nodded.

"They will surely try do delay us near the pass through the mountains", Marcus said. "It will allow the legions in Transsilvania time to mobilise."

We wished to travel fast, yet it was important to ensure that we would not be trapped by the legions. At five mile intervals, Bradakos tasked warriors to fill a portion of the ditch using the earthen rampart. Our barbarians used the tools left behind by the fleeing auxiliaries.

Hostilius was requested to oversee this, as he had the most experience with earthworks.

We had travelled less than ten miles when the king called a rest. Hostilius left us to oversee the destruction of a section of the rampart.

The vegetation was cleared fifty paces on each side of the road. Beyond the cleared area was the thickest, darkest forest I have ever seen. The day was unusually hot and humid so we took to the shade of the trees. Interestingly, our guide sat on his horse in the baking sun, twenty paces away, refusing to approach the treeline.

Gordas was about to draw his sword when the poor man went down on his knees, begging to be allowed to stay clear of the forest. Cai intervened on his behalf. "Leave be, Gordas. Man truly filled with fear. We need guide."

The Huns respected martial prowess above anything and Gordas had witnessed what the small easterner was capable of. He nodded and rode off to join his warband.

Ignoring the altercation, I lay down on the cool, leaf-covered ground, closed my eyes, and stretched out. Moments later I heard Pezhman's voice.

"Primus Pilus Hostilius asks that you join him on the wall, lord. He asks for the guide as well."

We followed Pezhman to where a horde of barbarians were congregated in front of the fortifications. In their midst, dismounted, stood a scowling Hostilius.

"We can't fill the ditch, Domitius."

"Why is that Primus Pilus?"

He motioned for me to follow him. I dismounted, passed the reins to a warrior and ascended the rampart to the wooden walkway at the top.

Strangely, there was no outer ditch.

The local guide was still with me, like a shadow. I assumed he felt less at risk trailing behind the lord, than left to the devices of the mob at the bottom of the ramp.

"I can't believe it, Domitius. Why would there be no ditch? I've never seen this before."

Hostilius turned to the scout. "Why no ditch?" he barked in Latin.

"Great general, ditch is not needed in this place." He pointed to where the dark trees grew at the edge of the forest. "We call it the 'Screaming Woods', lord general. The *Paduroaia* in there, the old hag of the forest." He clutched the amulet he wore around his neck to ward off the evil. "Many people do not believe. They go in, but never come back." He pointed again to somewhere yonder. "There 'Mad Forest'. Over there, 'Heinous Forest'. That one called 'Awful…'"

Hostilius stopped him mid-sentence. "We bloody well get the idea. That's enough."

"Yes general, sorry…"

Hostilius silenced him with a wave of his hand.

"This will take longer, Domitius. To create a breach, we will have to carry the soil farther, since there is no ditch to fill."

I rode to inform Bradakos, with the guide following close behind.

The legions had cleared sections of the forest to allow access to the river. The warriors were watering their horses and I patiently waited next to Simsek and my spare horse until it was my turn.

As soon as the horses had their fill, I rode back to where the warriors were labouring on the wall. I brought along a full waterskin for my friend.

He nodded his thanks and drank deeply from the skin with the ice cold water. "As hot as Hades out here, Domitius", he said, and wiped the sweat from his brow with the back of his hand.

"Let's go find some shade, Primus Pilus", I said. "Or are you afraid of the old woman of the forest?"

"Last old woman I was afraid of was my grandma. She was as mean as a bloody viper. Loved her to bits, though", he said.

I found it difficult to imagine Hostilius as a child. Sometimes, saying nothing is also a reply.

I mounted, with Hostillius falling in beside me. We trotted towards the brooding mogshade of the trees.

Simsek's ears pricked up as we walked our way into the gloom. I grabbed my strung bow from the saddle and three

134

arrows from the quiver. To my right, I heard Hostilius draw his gladius.

The hairs on the back of my neck raised and I felt a tingle down my spine. I was sure someone was watching us, but apart from moving shadows where the sun pierced the canopy, I could see no one.

I guided my horse forward to where the shivelights illuminated a slight clearing. An old woman dressed in black rags was picking mushrooms, her back bent with age.

She croaked, still going about her business: "You come to seek my advice, Scythian?"

A strange feeling of nausea rose from my stomach. I exchanged glances with an ashen Hostilius, who appeared decidedly uncomfortable, clutching his amulet.

The old crone peered over her shoulder, revealing sightless eyes.

"Beware the one who begs assistance, trust not the one who makes the peace", she hissed, then issued a toothless smile that did not fit the moment.

Her voice changed then, holding an edge of fragility. "The time is not yet upon us, illustrious one. When all hope is lost, Roman, return what was never yours to take."

"We have taken nothing, old woman", Hostilius replied flatly.

She cackled, as if laughing at a jest. "Oh, but you have, First Centurion."

She looked away. "Begone with you now, warriors. Leave before I change my mind", she sighed and started humming an eerie tune.

An inexplicable gust of air stirred the forest floor, causing the fallen leaves to flutter around her.

"Probably need to go see how they're getting on with the wall", Hostilius croaked.

"Race you there", I said.

* * *

Come evening, we camped in the vicinity of another abandoned fort, referred to as Albota by our guide. Yet again, the garrison had retreated, leaving enough spoils to keep the warriors occupied.

As was our habit, we all joined Bradakos around the fire. His guards had laid out furs while two sheep and a couple of wild fowl were slowly roasting over a wood fire.

The Roxolani king produced a large amphora of wine, of excellent quality I might add.

Gordas emptied his cup and held it out to a servant to refill. "I sent men to hunt boar earlier, reliable warriors. They have disappeared, as if the forest have swallowed them."

He turned to Hostilius. "I heard the guide tell you things earlier. Something about an evil that lives within the trees."

"Old womans' tales, my friend", the Primus Pilus replied.

Gordas shrugged and took another swallow.

Chapter 17 – Tarbus

The Road leading to the Arges River was an up and down affair. We were slowly but surely ascending through the foothills of the Western Carpathian Mountains. Our destination, the pass between Rucar and Bran. This route would give us access to the rich plateau of Transsilvania.

The Romans had constructed a magnificent wooden bridge across the river. An auxiliary fort, built on the northern bank, guarded the passage across.

Our scouts reported no Roman activity on our side of the river.

"They've run away, Domitius. Mark my words. I have spoken to the scout. There are places where the river can be crossed on horseback, so it is of no use to try and hold the bridge. The last thing they want is to be surrounded by barbarians."

It turned out that Hostilius was right and we spent the night on the northern bank of the Arges River.

True to my word, I released the villager guides before we crossed the river. They each carried a bulging purse filled with looted Roman coin as payment for services rendered.

As I watched the peasants skulk away, I noticed Gordas sitting close by on his horse, eyeing me with an amused expression.

"Waste of good gold, Eochar." He followed them with a longing stare. "I can still put arrows through them. At least they will die rich men."

"Forget them. Let us see what Bradakos is up to", I said, and steered Simsek to the bridge.

Little did we know that all was not well. The first hint was the raised voices discernible above the normal sounds of an army making camp.

"You are not my king, Roxolani", I heard someone growl forcefully, accentuating every word.

"We will settle this the old way, with swords, before the gods", came the reply of a familiar voice as we rounded the last of the smaller tents surrounding that of the king's.

Bradakos and Tarbus were facing each other, two paces separating them. My mentor and his bodyguards all had their hands on the hilts of their swords. The king of the Carpiani and his contingent had adopted the same pose.

I realised that within moments violence would be unleashed, so I uttered the wisest words that came to mind. "Good evening, my lords."

Bradakos and Tarbus both turned their gaze towards me and I continued. "The last of the men have crossed the river, lords. What are your orders?"

All gaped at me, stunned at my foolish interruption of the standoff between the kings.

Tarbus realised that he was outnumbered and decided to salvage the situation.

"I will do as I deem fit, Roxolani. I am not your lapdog to command. This is not finished." He turned on his heel and marched off in the direction of the Carpiani camp.

Bradakos remained as he was. He breathed deeply for a while, trying to douse the red-hot rage.

When he succeeded in calming himself, he turned to me, his anger still not fully under control. "I wanted to fight him, Eochar. Why in the name of the gods did you interfere?"

"Really?" I said. "My apologies, I didn't notice", I added.

The king scowled.

Just then Hostilius arrived with a sizeable amphora slung over his shoulder. "Look what I found."

He studied the serious faces staring back at him.

"What's the matter?" He sighed and placed the amphora on the ground. "Please don't tell me I've missed out on something again."

In any event, we managed to calm the king and soon Marcus, Vibius and Cai joined us around the fire. When all was present Bradakos shared the tale.

"Tarbus came to see me as soon as my tent had been erected. He told me that he was willing to fight at our side, if it proved necessary, to gain access to the pass that leads to Transsilvania."

"How nice of him", Hostilius added, and refilled his cup.

The king nodded. "I told him that it was expected of us to fight side by side, and that he was not doing me a favour. I reminded him of the blood oath."

"I invited him to a council of war so that we could make a joint decision on our course of action once we reach the land beyond the forest."

The king shook his head. "I don't know why, but he became angry then. He accused me of causing dissent within his ranks, turning his men against him."

Bradakos was nobody's plaything. As he retold the story, I could see the anger rising, his hand moving to the hilt of his sword.

"He said that he was tired of dancing to the tune of the Roxolani and the Huns. If and when we reach Transsilvania, he would go his own way."

"Eochar, were it not for your arrival, I would have challenged him to single combat."

Cai spoke wise words. "In face of enemy, not fight among self. Reconcile is best. Save anger for later."

Bradakos was no fool. He nodded in acknowledgement of Cai's advice. Then he turned to me and explained what he required.

I gestured for one of the Roxolani guards to approach and gave him a verbal message to be delivered to the Carpiani camp.

When we had eaten our fill of the abundance of wild meat and looted food, I left the fireside and walked off into the night. Hostilius insisted on accompanying me. Gordas had to be restrained, as he had failed to curtail his wine intake and would be more of a liability.

Sentries greeted us when we reached the Roman bridge across the Arges River. We walked east one hundred paces until we could discern a dark shape waiting on the bank.

"Greetings, Lord Eochar", came the whisper from the darkness.

"I am glad that you came, Thiaper", I said, and clasped his arm. Hostilius followed suit.

"Word has surely reached you of the altercation between Tarbus and Bradakos?" I asked.

"It is all that the men are talking about, lord", was his answer.

Gossip spreads faster than wildfire within an army.

I remained quiet, as he surely knew the reason for the meeting. Thiaper continued: "It started years ago, lord, when you captured the Carpiani warband and forced the king to provide foederati for the Persian campaign, but recently it has become worse."

He looked around as if to make certain no one was eavesdropping, and lowered his voice another level.

"Our warriors see how their Roxolani counterparts are treated by king Bradakos. He gifts his warriors a generous share of the loot and treats them with respect. It is not the way of Tarbus. The men are unhappy and Tarbus blames your king. He calls him a peasant who has won the crown. A puppet of the Huns, lord."

His words angered me, and I had to breathe deeply. My hand went to my sword involuntarily. My actions did not go unnoticed.

A nervous Thiaper whispered. "I do not share the views of the king, lord, but I will stand by him. He has not given me reason to defy him. My wish is for the Carpiani and Roxolani to fight side by side."

I nodded, taking my hand off the hilt. "We desire the same thing, Thiaper."

"There is one other thing, lord", he said. "The king has spoken of his wish to raid the Roman gold mines in the west of Transsilvania. His mind is set. Maybe, if he is allowed to do this, his mood will improve."

Hostilius interjected. "The Romans are clever bastards, Thiaper. This is what they will expect. Best is not to go near the gold mines."

I placed my hand on Hostillius's arm, to silence him. "We will talk to king Bradakos, Thiaper."

Chapter 18 – Jidova

We rode north on the morrow, following the Roman road which ascended to the highlands through a broad river valley. The sides of the road were heavily forested with oak and hornbeam, as were the slopes. To minimise the chance of being ambushed, the Romans had cleared the trees eighty paces on both sides, allowing the horde of horsemen to travel thirty abreast with ease.

I rode at the head of the Roxolani contingent, alongside Bradakos. We trailed behind the Carpiani who formed the vanguard on the day.

"It is a thoughtful gesture", I said.

My friend, the king, turned to me, his face drawn in a confused expression. "What are you talking about?"

"Allowing the Carpiani to be the vanguard, to ride in the place of honour", I said.

Bradakos laughed out loud. "No Eochar, I suggested that they ride up front because I don't trust them. I prefer to have Tarbus where I can see him, rather than at my back."

I shared the information I obtained from Thiaper then, a scowl forming on the face of the king that increased in severity as I progressed with the story.

"Puppet of the Huns, eh?" he hissed.

For a while we rode in silence, the king's brooding mood somehow spoiling the awe-inspiring beauty of the valley.

When he had digested my words, he said: "I will give my blessing to Tarbus and his Carpiani to go their own way once we enter Transsilvania, if it is his wish. Even if the Carpiani win much richer loot than us, it is preferable to a full-scale battle between the tribes, which will surely be the case if we remain together."

"I agree", I said.

I reached into my saddlebag and produced the itinerary I had gained from the study of the Roman officer. "I have studied the Roman documents. I have a few ideas of my own regarding loot."

"I'm listening", he replied, grinning like a wolf.

* * *

The army travelled a considerable distance that day, close to thirty miles.

We camped near another deserted fort along the Roman limes, called Jidova.

Bradakos was still brooding and Gordas had to settle some or other dispute among his commanders. It allowed me the time to spend a relaxed evening with my Roman friends and Cai.

The deserted Roman forts and the absence of any Roman resistance worried me. I shared these concerns with my comrades.

"Rome may be many things. Stupid not one of them", Cai said.

Marcus nodded. "Romans are clever and resourceful." He grinned. "Like us."

He took another swallow from the looted red and continued. "They will try and stop us before we get to the mountain pass. Of that I am certain."

"If it were me, I would set up an ambush", Hostilius said, and stuffed another handful of olives into his mouth. While chewing he continued. "And I would use artillery. Probably scorpion bolt throwers 'cause they are easy to deploy."

"These barbarians are good fighters", added Vibius, "but they have been lulled into a false sense of security. They think that Rome fears them. We know better. We know what the legions are capable of."

"Best is to put on boots of enemy. Become enemy. Think like enemy. Then find way to beat them", Cai added.

We dined on looted olives and cheese, dried salted meat and a smooth red.

Although we retired early, I had trouble falling asleep. Cai's words milled around inside my head. I became a Roman again in my mind, and worked out what they would do.

Something else was weighing down on me. Revenge. Or rather the lack thereof.

After the murder of my father and the destruction of my home, I had imagined that Arash would allow me the opportunity to exact revenge on Philip the Arab and his brother Priscus. Yet, I have been led further away from Rome. I realised that Nik's only wish would be for me to be happy, but still, I longed to get even.

I prayed to Arash to allow me to fulfil my destiny, whatever it may be. I told him then that I would accept his decision, even if it meant that I would never again enter the lands of Rome.

In hindsight, I think Arash was waiting for me to place my revenge of Priscus and the Arab in his hands. Revenge exacted by a man can be a terrible thing, but in the hands of a god it is worse.

Chapter 19 – Rucar

When Vibius kicked my foot, it was still dark inside the tent. And I was dead tired, feeling as if I had slept less than a watch.

"The scouts found the Romans at Rucar, eh?" I said, and wiped the sleep from my eyes.

Vibius stared at me for a couple of heartbeats with his mouth agape. "Arash told me", I answered and shrugged.

"The kings have requested our council", he said as he assisted me to don my Scythian scale armour. I strapped on my weapons and exited the tent where a warrior was waiting for me, holding a saddled Simsek by the reins. Nobility has its advantages.

My friends and I rode to the tent of Bradakos. Gordas was waiting outside, clearly excited about the prospect of battle.

"I have never fought the Romans, Eochar. Before the end of the day, Roman scalps will decorate my saddle." He pointed to the gladius strapped to my side. "I will make sure I kill an officer. They carry the best weapons and I want a long dagger like you have."

"It's not a dagger, Gordas. It's a shortsword. The Romans call it a gladius."

He eyed me skeptically. "Whatever you say, Eochar."

Just then the flap opened and guards ushered us into the tent of the king. Servants handed us each a cup of hot salted mare's milk as we entered.

To my surprise, Tarbus was already inside, wearing a smug expression.

Bradakos enlightened us. "Yesterday evening, after you departed, our advance scouts returned. They found the Romans fifteen miles north of here. They are hiding behind an earthen rampart fortified by a ditch. The scouts estimate that the Romans number only three thousand."

Tarbus announced the decision of the kings. "The brave warriors of the Carpiani will chase the Romans from their hiding place. As payment, our warriors will claim the loot."

I couldn't help but wonder how much of the loot would end up in the saddlebags of Tarbus.

The Carpiani king clasped arms with Bradakos and departed, his smug expression intact.

After Tarbus left, Bradakos exhaled slowly, as if he had been holding his breath for ever.

I recognized the familiar scent of cannabis smoke.

My mentor answered my enquiring stare. "I had the shaman prepare me a smoke tent earlier", he said. "It helped."

Bradakos's drugged state explained his puzzling calm demeanour in the presence of the Carpiani king.

Hostilius motioned with his head towards the opening of the tent through which Tarbus had just departed. "He is underestimating the Romans, which is never good for one's health."

The Roxolani king gave a small nod. "I granted his every request for the sake of unity. Let us hope that he does not find death in the same place he is seeking glory and loot."

Cai sniffed the air. "Smoke of 'ma' plant help foretell future. Also turn man into poet."

The king scowled.

He motioned for us to sit down on the soft furs spread out on the ground.

"There are none better qualified than you to advise me on how to proceed", the king said.

I emptied my cup, savouring the taste of the warm milk. "We would speak with the scouts, Bradakos."

Before long, two Roxolani scouts were seated opposite us in the spacious tent of the king.

As was expected, they addressed the man of highest rank in the room. "Lord king, we followed the stone road north, keeping the river, eh... stream, on our right. When we reached the foothills of the mountains we turned east, past the quarry, as Lord Eochar told us to do."

I traced their movements using the Roman itinerary.

Looking up from the scroll, I nodded in acceptance of their words.

The scouts stared at me with confused expressions.

Gordas stepped in, enlightening them. "Lord Eochar has captured the magic scroll from the Romans. The markings tell him whether your words are accurate."

The scouts suddenly appeared decidedly nervous. "Everyone knows that the god speaks to you, lord, but we did not realise that you also practise the sacred art of divination."

They inclined their heads in respect. I scowled at Gordas who wore a smug look on his scarred face.

"When we reached the stream the locals call the Dambovita River, we turned north, up the valley", the scout continued. "We followed the Roman road and passed four of the Roman road stones, so we travelled four miles, lord."

They looked at me with childlike expressions, expecting me to divine the accuracy of their words.

152

I realised that to play along would be the least problematic. "Your words carry no deceit", I said.

Sighing with relief, the head scout carried on. "The valley became steeper and narrower as we continued, lord. The sides of the valley are dark forests, lord, with thick undergrowth. Men on horseback cannot travel within it. Maybe men on foot, lord, but it would not be easy."

"There is a place where the valley narrows and the river flows close to the treeline on the eastern slope, lord. There the Romans have dug a ditch with an earthen rampart at the back."

"How wide is the valley?" Marcus queried.

"It is only two hundred and fifty paces wide, Roman lord."

Bradakos dismissed the scouts. "You have done well and will be rewarded."

After they left, Hostilius spoke first. "The Romans will line the wall with artillery. I have seen some of the bolts they left behind at the forts in their eagerness to leave. They look to be of the size they use in carroballistae. Bloody nasty piece of work, a carroballista. Built to be hauled about on a heavy cart and operated by a full contubernium. Can throw a bolt the size of a pilum as far as four hundred paces. I've used them myself in battle a couple of times. One of those bolts hit you, you burst open like a ripe plum, truth be told."

153

"Thank you, Centurion, I think we get the picture", Marcus replied.

"I just say it as it is, Tribune", Hostilius said.

Marcus acknowledged him with a curt nod.

Strangely, they all shifted their gaze to me. I remained quiet until Hostilius asked: "So what is the plan, Domitius?" He paused to take in my expression. "And don't look so surprised. The god of war speaks to you, not to us!"

I didn't have a plan at hand, but Gordas came to the rescue. "Maybe chanting some of the spells on the scroll will work?"

In any event, I was unable to come up with a concrete plan, although Arash planted an idea in the back of my mind.

"Gordas, I would like to have two of the local peasant farmers brought to me."

"Consider it done", he said and left the tent immediately, relishing the idea of terrorising the local populace.

Bradakos concluded the meeting as we heard the sound of thousands of Carpiani striking camp. "All we can do for the time being is to watch the Carpiani assault. There is no way I can dissuade Tarbus. He will attack the fortifications no matter what. If I stand in his way, he might attack the Roxolani instead."

I shrugged. "You never know, he may break through and win a great victory."

* * *

The afternoon was mild and overcast. I relaxed in the saddle, relieved to be a spectator for a change.

I was surrounded by my companions, although Gordas was absent. The Hun and his men were without a doubt scouring the countryside in an attempt to ferret a few unfortunate peasants from the holes they were hiding in. Bradakos was with his noble commanders, who were keen to watch the imminent battle in the company of their king.

I had very little concern for the welfare of Tarbus, although I regretted the fact that he would be exposing his men to the terrible Roman artillery. I said a silent prayer to Arash for my friend, Thiaper, who would no doubt lead the attack from the front.

We watched from an elevated position, a sparsely treed copse bordering the left side of the valley. The Romans were six hundred paces distant, their red shields lining the top of the rampart which was fortified with a wooden palisade. It was too far away to establish whether stakes lined the ditch, but knowing the Romans' attention to detail, I already knew the answer.

The Roman soldiers screened the ballistae from view, but there was little doubt in my mind that the clusters of men, at regularly spaced intervals, were the contubernia crews manning these devices.

Hostilius confirmed my suspicions. "I count twenty-three ballistae, one every ten paces."

The Romans had chosen their position wisely. The limited frontage allowed by the narrow valley meant that the advantage created by the greater numbers of the barbarians, was negated. The Carpiani would have to attack in packed, deep ranks. This was the perfect scenario for the ballistae to cause maximum destruction. The artillery was reasonably accurate, but ineffective against an enemy spread out across the field of battle.

Tarbus's barbarians were filling the narrow valley five hundred paces from the Romans, safely out of range of the ballistae.

There would be no clear strategy, apart from overwhelming the enemy with sheer numbers. The Romans watched from the wall in stoic silence while the barbarians shouted and screamed, gathering courage in the process.

The Carpiani warriors were milling about, with groups of riders joining from the rear. Then, as if a dam wall burst, they charged the Romans in dense ranks.

As one the ballistae spat their bolts at the front ranks of the charging Carpiani. I watched as a bolt, shot almost horizontally, struck a horse at full gallop. The dart skewered the neck of the horse, imbedding in the torso of the rider. The horse was killed instantly, the force of the strike throwing it to the side and causing it to collide with the horse next to it. Both horses went down in a tangle of limbs. Most of the trailing riders managed to avoid the mess but one could not.

Before the third rider went down, the crew manning the ballista reloaded. This time the bolt passed through the torso of a warrior and affixed the leg of a second to his horse. For a moment I turned my head away. It was no battle, it was a slaughter.

When the Romans were within arrow range, the Carpiani released volleys at the enemy ranks lining the top of the rampart. The Romans ducked behind the palisade and quickly organized themselves in the testudo formation with their curved shields protecting them from above. They had another surprise for the horse barbarians. From behind the legionaries, auxiliary archers released deadly volleys of arrows into the packed ranks of the lightly armoured Carpiani.

The first of the Carpiani reached the fortifications. They jumped from their horses and charged the enemy, wielding swords and spears. When the ditch and the base of the rampart was thick with charging barbarians, I heard the faint command of the centurion bellowing at the top of his voice. "Release pila."

Thousands of spears struck the barbarians, effectively annihilating the first wave of the attack.

The ballista crews knew their business and each device spat a bolt every twenty heartbeats. The middle and back ranks of the Carpiani were bunched up, allowing the ballistae to slaughter them at will. The Romans did not have it all their way, though. I saw dead legionaries slumped over the rampart where the odd arrow had penetrated minute gaps between shields.

The second wave of attackers were through the ditch when another volley of pila broke their charge.

At one point along the wall, the Carpiani had successfully scaled the palisade, gaining a foothold on top of the rampart. I saw the reserve force of the Romans trotting toward the breach, followed by fierce fighting. Before long, Carpiani corpses were thrown over the palisade, rolling into the ditch. The Romans had regained the rampart.

Then, suddenly, it was over. The Carpiani turned tail, leaving the field.

An almighty cheer erupted from the Roman lines. In that moment I did not view them as my countrymen, but as the men in league with the murderers of my father.

Hundreds of mutilated bodies of men and horses littered the ground in front of the fortifications.

"Hate to say it", Hostilius said, "but I could have told them exactly what would happen."

Acceptance of defeat has ever been difficult for me. I turned my horse and went to find Gordas.

Chapter 20 – Hostages

On the positive side, I heard that my friend Thiaper had survived. In addition, the Hun commander managed to find four local peasants.

They were caught in the act of stealing a pair of the Huns' spare horses.

"I rescued them", Gordas stated proudly. "The warriors were about to exact punishment."

"What kind of punishment?" I queried.

"They probably would have ripped their arms off", he answered earnestly, "but because they stole horses, it might have been worse."

I found it difficult to imagine what kind of punishment could have been worse, but opted not to ask.

I turned to face the four men, or rather, two oldsters and two boys who could not have been older than seventeen summers.

My appearance was far from Roman hence I could see their surprise when I addressed them in Latin.

"Are you aware that you are dead already?" I asked.

One of the oldsters nodded, too afraid to speak in the presence of the strange barbarian lord.

"But I have the power to let you live again", I said.

I took two gold coins from my purse and handed it to Gordas. "Give this as compensation to the warriors who have been wronged. I am taking these men."

"Come with me", I said and walked away.

They followed, reluctantly at first, not knowing what horrible fate I had in mind for them. That is until Gordas fell in behind them, which served as a reminder of the alternative.

First we spoke about the weather. Once I had enough of a grasp, I fed them well and readied the oldsters for the mission. They would leave as soon as darkness descended. The two boys would remain as hostages, their fate sealed should their fathers fail.

I sought out the Roxolani king to share my plan. I found Bradakos sitting with his face in his hands inside his tent.

There was only one possible explanation.

"Tarbus?" I asked.

He sighed. "I am past getting angry. Talking to him now fills me with despair."

He filled his cup from a small amphora and emptied it in one gulp. "We will break our men on these Roman walls, Eochar, until we start fighting one another. A full-scale confrontation

161

with Tarbus is unavoidable. He came to me and blamed us for his defeat. His said that you and your Roman friends were aware of the ballistae, but chose not to warn him. Not that he would have listened to reason."

I put my hand on his armoured shoulder. Touching the person of a king without permission would normally mean death, but Bradakos and I were closer than brothers.

"Come, brother. Sit. Listen to the message of Arash."

When I was done sharing my plan, it was nearly dark and time to act.

Bradakos summoned his two best scouts and I explained what I required.

Once I was certain that they understood, I made them repeat the instructions given to them.

"Go when it is dark", I said. "Use the river and the forest. Take along sufficient cold fare for seven days. Do not show yourselves until the appointed time."

"We are only four men, lord. We will not be noticed."

I turned to the oldsters. "I will reward you with Roman loot and the lives of your sons if you are successful."

The one oldster, now emboldened, replied: "We will not fail you, highborn lord. We hate the Romans, we do. Many seasons past, we were a tribe of brave warriors. Rome has reduced us to this."

I was sure that he would have said the opposite if he faced a Roman, but I nodded and left him with a departing threat. "Do not disappoint me."

Answering Bradakos's summons, Gordas arrived.

"Are the skills of the Hun warriors needed?" he queried.

I explained all.

"Remember Gordas, your warriors need to mark the positions so that they will be able to find it with their eyes closed."

Gordas smiled and spoke in the way one would to a worried child. "These men are the best. They will find their way without markings, but if it makes you feel better, they will mark it."

"It will make me feel better", I said.

* * *

The fourth day started out hot and humid and it stayed that way until late afternoon when a cool breeze blew in from the east.

There had been incidents between warriors of the tribes, no doubt caused by the strife between the kings and exacerbated by the defeat of the Carpiani. Something had to be done to quell the growing tension in the barbarian camp.

The two young horse thieves were held in a tent in the middle of the Hun camp. For obvious reasons, they did not even consider venturing outside. Gordas had posted three guards, although it was probably to ensure the safety of the boys, rather than to keep them from escaping.

As I bent over and entered the tent, I was met with broad smiles.

"It will be tomorrow, lord."

"Are you sure?"

I received an answer typical of boys their age, who knew it all. "We can smell it in the air, lord, it is a certainty", the younger one said. The older boy nodded his agreement.

Walking back to my tent, I could not help but think that I would be gambling men's lives based on the words of mere boys.

Yet, the conditions were as described by the oldsters. I would roll the dice... and pray to Fortuna.

Chapter 21 – The Girl

Hostillius squinted, trying his best to peer through the thick white fog rolling over the plain from the towering peaks above us.

"The locals believe the fog is a girl, a god-child, locked away in a mountain cave for her sins. Her brothers are the clouds. When the gods wish it, they let her out for a while. She creeps along the ground then, ashamed to show her face, and to rise to where her brothers live."

Gordas was not to be outdone. "My people believe that when the fog descends, the evil creatures who dwell in the forest, hungry for souls, spill out onto the plains to …"

Before my lesson in folklore could be completed, a Hun warrior materialised from the fog.

The inability to see farther than ten paces makes one prone to nervousness. All of our hands jerked to our swords at his sudden arrival, which caused the scout to grin at his attempt at stealth.

He inclined his head to his commander. "The warriors are in place, general. What are your orders?"

Gordas spoke softly. "Lord Eochar will go with you. It is he who will command."

Behind us, thousands of Roxolani warriors were waiting next to their mounts, making last minute adjustments to the tack of their horses. Some were stringing bows, others searching for the best fletched arrow. The Carpiani tribesmen were absent, their king unwilling to partake.

"We will wait until you send for us, Eochar", Bradakos said. "Then the Roxolani will unleash the wrath of the Scythians."

Cai remained in camp. Vibius, Marcus and Hostilius would accompany me.

The scout motioned for us to follow him. "Best is we do not talk from now on, lord. I will walk slowly, for the sake of your Roman friends."

Days before, concealed by the darkness of night, the Hun scouts had marked the exact positions of each carroballista stationed on the Roman earthen rampart. I had ordered the construction of forty-six wooden ladders, twice the number of the ballistae on the wall.

My strategy was simple. Forty paces from each ballista, in front of the ditch, thirty Huns would congregate, invisible to the Romans due to the thick fog. Each group would carry two ladders to enable them to cross the stake-filled ditch, once their arrows had eliminated the crews manning the ballistae.

Small noises were of no concern as the vermin that normally sheltered in the woods were forever feasting on the Carpiani corpses close to the wall, from where their comrades were unable to collect them. The negative was the sickening stench of death all around.

There was another element to my plan. The fathers of the peasant boys we held hostage would appear in the Roman camp, begging for assistance, as their home farther north up the valley had been attacked by hundreds of barbarians. Any Roman commander worth his salt would at least take some men from the rampart as a precaution against an attack from the rear. It was close to impossible for an enemy force to have circled around the Roman position due to the near impenetrable forests, but history is littered with the corpses of commanders who believed that the enemy could not accomplish the impossible. Take Hannibal's crossing of the Alps as an example.

In any event, I would wait for a watch past sunrise for the Romans to withdraw men. If nothing had happened by then, we would attack.

I was becoming impatient, convinced that the fog was lifting, which would mean death by a ballista bolt should we be seen. I stole a glance at Hostilius at my side, who gave a small shake of his head which meant: "The bloody peasants have let you down, what did you expect?"

167

I scowled and decided to wait two hundred more heartbeats.

Then, louder than expected, came the command from the gloom in front of us. "Second, third and fourth century, follow Centurion Petronius. Make sure each of you take three pila. Rest of you, spread out."

Again, the time passed excruciatingly slow as I waited for the legionaries to leave the rampart.

I touched Gordas's arm. The Hun grinned, passed the signal down the line and thirty Huns each took four arrows in their draw hands, their laminated recurve bows drawn to full extension.

Gordas howled like a wolf, a signal for the other Hun bands as well as the Roxolani. The armour-piercing arrows were deadly at one hundred paces, but at forty paces they were a horror to behold. "Whack!" Thirty arrows struck as one, each with the power of a war hammer. Men screamed terribly and I could hear dull thuds as some, staggering from the impact, fell backwards from the rampart. Again, again and again, the deadly arrows struck within less than four heartbeats. All along the length of the fortification, the same scene played out as men screamed and moaned. But the Romans were no fools. The ones who survived would now be hiding behind shields or crouching down behind the rampart.

The Huns released another four-arrow volley when the earth began to vibrate with the impact of thousands of hooves. The Roxolani released their arrows virtually straight up in the air, causing an arrow-rain to descend on the Romans, falling near vertically from the sky. Four volleys of arrows afforded the Huns time to cross the ditch. Due to the completeness of the surprise, the Romans never had a chance to release their pila before the Urugundi were upon them. I was next to Gordas, who cupped his hand, providing me with a foothold to vault over the palisade. I landed on the rampart. Simultaneously a Roman spear was thrust at my head. My gladius was in my hand as I knew it would be close quarter work, and I diverted the strike. I turned my shoulder into the shield and shoved the Roman off the rampart. Another, a centurion, crouched down low with the top edge of his shield angled backwards. I mimicked his action, crouched down and met him shield to shoulder. He tried to unbalance me using the bottom edge of his shield. The officer was brutally strong and inched me towards the edge of the rampart, his gladius held behind his shield, ready to strike at the most opportune moment.

From nowhere, Gordas's lasso ripped his shield to the side and I skewered the Roman's neck with my gladius.

But there is a reason why the Roman Empire ruled most of the known world. The disciplined legionaries regrouped. I grabbed the centurion's shield to face the four Roman soldiers bearing down on me in a neatly dressed line, moving along the top of the rampart. Gordas stood with only his sword, extremely confident. Thankfully Hostilius pushed him aside and fell in next to me with his looted shield. Marcus and Vibius followed suit.

To trained legionaries, it must have appeared laughable. Four barbarians trying to wield unfamiliar weapons. But they were unaware of the fact that we had honed our skills for years, training daily, as close as brothers.

We stood, waiting for them. The first rank approached confidently, ready to dispatch the barbarian rabble. Hostilius gave the command and we ran forward when our adversaries were but five paces away. We angled our shields downward at the moment of impact, lifting the bottom edges of the legionaries' shields. At the same moment, we went down on one knee and stabbed for the feet. When I felt the impact and heard a scream, I propelled my shield upward with tremendous force and thrust into an abdomen with my sword, piercing mail. Gordas and the Huns supported us from behind, but we were fighting a losing battle. The well-armoured and trained legionaries would wear us down, eventually.

That is until I heard a panicked scream in Latin from down in the Roman camp. "Save yourselves, the Scythians are among us."

The fog was burning away and I saw hundreds of Roxolani riding through the Roman camp, shooting at legionaries from the saddle, or simply bowling over the one or two who tried to make a stand.

During the confusion of the attack, after we had eliminated the Roman artillery, five hundred of the Roxolani warriors, commanded by Bradakos, headed for the river on our right flank that anchored the Roman fortifications. The mounted Roxolani waded upstream along the far bank of the river, approaching the Roman camp from the rear. Their advance, under cover of the fog and the noise of battle, went unnoticed by the distracted Romans.

By that time, the Roman commanders had figured that the warning from the peasants was a ruse. They sent the men back to their original stations in order to drive the barbarians from the wall. Unopposed, Bradakos and his men attacked from the rear, crushing the Roman resistance.

The Huns and Roxolani slew many Romans, but some escaped to the forest, where pursuit on horseback was unwise, if not impossible.

Chapter 22 – Passage

The thick white fog was only a memory, burned away by a blazing hot sun.

Miraculously the two local oldsters survived. I gave the order for them to be rewarded with gold. The Huns would send them on their way, accompanied by their sons.

Marcus and Vibius returned to camp while my barbarian friends were stripping the corpses of anything of value, whooping with joy when they found some or other trinket.

I was dead tired and wished for nothing more than to take a swim in the icy water of the river, which originated high up in the Carpathians.

Arriving at the river, I noticed that it was not as clear as I expected it to be, due to the Roxolani horses churning up the mud upstream. Nonetheless, I stripped my armour and dived into the cool water, remaining under the surface for as long as I could hold my breath.

The battle and planning had sapped my strength, but I was also mentally exhausted. Not long before I had been a Roman legionary, now I was fighting on the side of the barbarians, killing Romans. Was I a traitor to Rome? Did the fact that the emperor wished me dead and tried to murder my family justify my actions?

The water slowly ran clearer as the murk drifted downstream, along with my troubles. I realised then that whatever I thought did not matter. My destiny lay in the hands of Arash. The god would decide.

I dived down again and remained submerged in the cool water until I was forced to surface, gasping for air. I felt clean and invigorated.

The feeling lasted less than ten heartbeats. An acrid smell carried on the breeze blowing down the narrow valley. I turned my gaze north to where black smoke spiralled to the heavens.

It was obvious, the wooden Roman fort at Rucar had been set to the torch.

Bradakos had forbidden his warriors to burn Roman forts. I was sure that the legion stationed in Transsilvania would have been informed of our presence in the Rucar-Bran area, but there was no need to give away our exact location.

There could be only one explanation. Tarbus.

I was not the only one who had noticed the smoke.

On my arrival, I found that my friends had already joined the king in his tent. "For one trained in way of Dao, take very long to smell fire", Cai chastised me.

Bradakos was livid. "I think that Tarbus has taken the Carpiani through the pass into Transsilvania", he growled. "And let me tell you, I pray to the gods that he has, because if I find him, there will be blood."

Gordas appeared in the doorway of the tent. He gestured with his head to where the fort was burning. "My scouts have arrived with reports but I wish to see with my own eyes."

"So would I", said Hostilius, who was echoing all our thoughts.

The small fort, or rather what remained of it, was cleverly built in an area that provided natural elevation. It was little more than an earthen wall topped with a twelve-feet-high wooden palisade. On the inside, a wooden walkway allowed the garrison to defend the walls.

I tried to make sense of the gruesome scene when Marcus interrupted. He pointed to twenty men, still wearing their full legionary garb, impaled on stakes. "They must have sought sanctuary inside the fort, but the Carpiani caught them in the open."

I thought them all dead, but one man uttered a low moan. Gordas mercifully silenced him with an arrow.

Marcus continued, pointing at the charred remains of legionaries nailed to the outside of the palisade. "They either surrendered when the fort was set alight, or maybe the Carpiani gained access?"

"There is no honour in this", Hostilius hissed. "Word will get out. It always does. Rome will have revenge, it is their way, even if it takes them a hundred years."

"The fire would have taken the spirits of the Roman warriors to Tengri", Gordas said, and pointed to the corpses still elevated on the stakes. "We should give their bodies to the fire god as well. They died a terrible death in this life so they will get a place of honour in the next."

Gordas dismounted, took an axe from his saddle and chopped down the first of the stakes. I assisted Bradakos with the gory job of moving the corpses to the intact part of the fort which would soon go up in flames. Hostilius, Marcus, Vibius and Cai all lended a hand.

It was dusk when the last of the logs in the palisade collapsed onto the bodies, sending a shower of smoke and orange sparks up into the heavens.

Gordas nodded with satisfaction. "It is a sign. The gods have accepted the spirits of the Roman warriors. They are in the presence of Tengri, purified by the fire." He turned his horse and headed back to camp. We all followed in silence.

I could not help but feel partly responsible for the gruesome torture endured by the unfortunate legionaries. Strangely, the act of labouring with the corpses followed by the burning of the bodies served as a kind of atonement. Just maybe Gordas was right and the fire purified us as well?

None of us were in the mood for company. I retired to my tent, cleaned my weapons and armour, then wolfed down some dried deer meat before I collapsed on the furs.

Before dawn I was disturbed from a deep, dreamless sleep by the noise of warriors stirring to strike camp.

Cai rose early to prepare a thick porridge of millet and wheat. We stood around the fire, each having been handed a bowl and a spoon.

"What happens now?" enquired Vibius.

"I believe we will cross the mountains to gain access to the rich lands of Transsilvania", Marcus replied. "But the decision lies with the Roxolani king."

"What about the Carpiani?" Vibius asked.

"Those bloody idiots will probably do something stupid", Hostilius said. "Tarbus's greed will get them all killed soon enough. If it were up to me, I would leave them be to get on with it."

"You know Bradakos well, Domitius. What will he do?" Hostilius asked.

"Bradakos will consult with us. Of that I am sure", I replied, taking a long swig of hot salted mare's milk.

I rolled my tent into a neat bundle and tied it to my packhorse together with my sleeping furs, spare clothing and cooking utensils. I was adjusting the straps to make sure that the weight was evenly distributed when a bodyguard of the king appeared.

"The king invites Lord Eochar and his companions to ride with him at the head of the army", he announced.

An invitation from a king is in actual fact an order so we followed the guard as soon as we had readied the horses.

Marcus and I rode alongside Bradakos with Hostilius, Vibius and Cai following in the second rank. We trailed behind a contingent of fifty bodyguards. These elite warriors were tasked to protect the king in case of an ambush, although it was highly unlikely, as many groups of mounted scouts left earlier to ensure there were no surprises along the way.

According to the itinerary, we would have to travel twenty miles along a winding road, built by the Romans to follow the natural contours of the hills and valleys.

We passed the charred remains of the fort at Rucar where the road turned east, snaking up a steep incline which forced us to slow the pace.

Bradakos gave me a sideways glance. "Tell me what you would do when we reach Transsilvania, if you in were in charge", he said, "and how you think the legions will respond."

I had studied the Roman itinerary during our travels north, and debated it many a time with my Roman friends.

"We believe that the legions will have a few objectives", I replied. "Emperor Traianus conquered Dacia to get hold of the gold mines. Firstly, they will protect the emperor's coin. Secondly, they will retain a strong presence in the larger cities."

Hostilius, who had been listening, nosed his horse in between Bradakos's and mine. "Not that Rome cares about the citizens, they wish to protect the trading stations and homes of the wealthy merchants, who just happen to be senators. If the rich and powerful become discontent, they will connive to stab the Arab in the back. Quite literally."

"Thirdly", Marcus continued, "they will do their best to trap us. They know we will eventually leave, so they are not that concerned about our presence in general. What the emperor desires is a victory of some kind. Something that he can take and turn into a triumph, a celebration of his military astuteness. Something that will make his name great."

"My friends are correct", I said.

"Tarbus has gone off to raid the gold mines", Bradakos said. "The legions will guard the major walled cities like Apulum. What remains for us? Do we chase around the countryside and loot grain and chickens from peasants?"

"No, my friend." I lifted the Roman itinerarium. "We have other ideas."

I gestured to the hills surrounding us. "The highlands of Transsilvania has very few plains, it is much like what you see around you: A network of fertile river valleys surrounded by densely forested hills. Many roads and pathways connect the areas. It will be a difficult task for the legions to trap us, if not impossible. Even the great Hadrianus found it difficult to pin down the Daci when he conquered these lands, all those years ago."

Just then, Gordas arrived with five of his warriors in tow. "Eochar, let us see whether my horse can still outrun Simsek."

"We will talk again around the fire tonight", Bradakos said. "Show the Hun what a Roxolani prince can do."

I grinned and kicked the Hun horse with my heels. Gordas knew what was coming and he was ready. He also rode a magnificent horse, the best the Hun breed had to offer. We raced past the Roxolani nobles, riding side by side for what seemed like miles, none able to overtake the other.

As if by agreement, we pulled on the reins, slowing down our horses to a walk.

"You ride like a Hun, Eochar", he said.

"And you like a Roxolani", I replied.

Chapter 23 – Apulum (June 245 AD)

It was later the same afternoon. We descended along a river valley which terminated in a narrow natural gateway. The passage between the hills was sixty paces wide, making it an ideal site for the Romans to delay our large army.

A scout arrived to report to Bradakos. "The land is empty lord, apart from riders who watched us from far away. They disappeared on our approach. At the other side of the stone gates lies a rich, fertile plain with a river and enough grazing for the horses."

The king dismissed the scout with a wave of his hand. "Let us make camp and rest." He turned to me. "You and your companions will dine with me tonight, Prince Eochar."

Before long we were seated around a raging fire next to the tent of the king. The abundance of ancient forests yielded wood of the best quality.

Hostilius tore a mouthful of juicy meat from a joint of mutton. He spoke while chewing. "Bloody best meat I had in weeks. Must be the coals they used to spit it over. The quality of the wood makes a huge difference."

He wiped the fatty juices from his beard with the back of his hand. "Those riders the scouts kept seeing on the horizon were probably exploratores. Auxiliaries. Huntsmen recruited by the Romans. They will keep their eyes on us so the legions will know where we are."

"Then we need to show them what they expect to see", I said.

Cai added. "Lucius of Da Qin speak true. Men see what expect to see. Wise general use against enemy."

Marcus used his palm to smooth a section of the sand next to the fire. He picked up a stick, drawing his dagger to sharpen one end.

He drew a crude circle in the soil. "This represents Transsilvania, circled by the Carpathian Mountains", he said, "and we are more or less here." He indicated a spot at the edge of the circle, toward the bottom on the right, and marked it with a cross.

Marcus drew another cross at the top of the circle, to the left. "This is Apulum, the capital of Transsilvania, larger than any of the cities along the Danube. Legio XIII Gemina is based here, along with the military command. Apulum protects the access to the passes that lead to the major gold mines in the mountains to the northwest."

He used the stick to make two indents in the sand, either side of Apulum.

"We will make them believe that we are heading for the gold mines. Rather, we will raid the iron mine to the south at Deva and the salt mine to the north of the capital, close to Potaissa."

Bradakos nodded. "Iron of quality is scarce in Scythia, as is salt. These commodities are nearly as valuable as gold."

"What about Tarbus?" asked Hostilius.

"Tarbus has chosen his path, Centurion. It has naught to do with us", Bradakos said.

"I disagree", I said, which drew a frown from Bradakos, followed by a scowl. Although we were all friends, to disagree with the king was still not acceptable.

"Let Tarbus follow his path, yes, but let us allow him to help us."

Bradakos slapped my back. "Tell us," he said.

So I did.

It turned out to be a fine evening. We made plans, then celebrated our progress with a feast. At last we had arrived, and all that remained was to pick the ripe fruit from the lands of Transsilvania. Or so we thought.

Our plan was simple. The Roxolani would advance at speed to the capital. Hot on the heels of Tarbus and the Carpiani horde.

The army would camp close to Apulum where at least a couple of cohorts of the XIII Gemina would defend the fortress.

The legions would be distracted, as the Carpiani would have moved past Apulum to gain access to the passes that lead to the gold mines, farther to the west. The Roxolani under Elmanos would harass the garrison and launch half-hearted attacks on the walls of the city. It would only be a diversion, of course.

We rode like only the Scythians and the Huns could, covering the one hundred and thirty miles in two days. We even outpaced the exploratores, some of them falling into the hands of the barbarians. Others simply abandoned their horses and melted into the forests.

Due to the speed of our advance, the Romans were not forewarned. On the afternoon of the second day, we camped within sight of the walls of Apulum on the eastern bank of the Mures River. To the east, our campsite was bordered by a series of low forested hills, which was why the site had been chosen.

Later, after we had set up camp and the light faded, I found Hostilius standing on the bank of the river, staring intently at the Roman legionary fortress less than a mile distant. The last rays of the sun, about to dip behind the Western Carpathians, silhouetted the Romans watching from the rampart.

"Still feels like I should be on those walls, Domitius", he sighed. "I gave them twenty bloody years of my life. What do I get in return?"

I knew it wasn't a question, so I let him speak. "Let me tell you. A kick in the arse, that's what."

He turned to me then, and growled, his anger visible. "I want blood as payment." He pointed to the low hill. "Not the blood of those Roman farm boys over there, Domitius, but the blood of Priscus and the Arab."

"There will be many of those boys standing between us and the men you want to get your hands on", I said.

"That's too bad for them then, eh?" He smiled, the anger suddenly gone. "Fortuna can be a bitch, Domitius."

* * *

Once darkness descended, we left the camp and moved into the treeline, in single file, led by a scout. At my back rode Cai, Hostilius, Gordas and close to a thousand Huns.

We walked our horses through near blackness for the best part of a double watch, in our full armour. Not that we expected to give battle, but ever tried riding through a forest at night?

185

The rider and horse to your front, passing through the trees, bend the branches. When they are clear, the branch whips back with a vengeance. The armour helps, as does inclining your head and turning it to the side, which protects the eyes.

Eventually we arrived at the deserted plain where we would spend the night. I was unscathed, save for a small gash on the bridge of my nose, which could have been my eye, were it not for Fortuna.

We ate dried meat and hard cheese, spoke little, lit no fires and slept next to our horses.

Cai woke me, kicking my foot. "Best rise, Lucius of Da Qin. Day wait for no one."

We rode at a canter for the first mile or two and crossed a stream the locals call the Sebes. We turned east, back into the Mures River Valley.

Gordas rode alongside me, grinning in anticipation. I nodded and grinned back.

The Hun balled his fist and waved it about above his head, howling. Soon a thousand Huns were thundering down the valley at breakneck speed. The need for stealth had passed.

The valley was five miles wide so I harboured no concerns that we could be trapped on our return. We kept the river and distant hills to our right.

The Primus Pilus possessed an uncanny sense of direction, which was probably the product of traversing unknown enemy territory countless times. It was near the middle of the day when Hostilius reined in and pointed to a milestone in the Roman road. "We have travelled thirty miles, Domitius, now we turn south." He pointed to the distant hills, while studying the itinerarium. "The mine is that way."

As we neared the area we knew to be the location of the mine, I noticed thin tendrils of smoke rising from the forested hills.

Cai, who rode beside me, noticed my inquisitive glance. "In Serica, peasants make charcoal. Chop down ancient trees, make much wood." He motioned with his hands to indicate a huge pile. "Pile wood, then cover with clay and soil. Burn for week. Sell to mine for iron furnace." He pointed to the woods. "Peasants here do same."

Before long the location of the mine was undisputable. Thick black smoke emanated from a hilly area two miles distant. I ordered a halt and gathered my friends. We rode to investigate, dismounting close to the crest of a hill which overlooked the mine. Fortunately there was enough cover in the form of shrubs, allowing us to lie down on our stomachs and study the area below.

Again, it was Cai who enlightened us. "Slaves mine iron with pick and axe from hole in ground, over there. Make big pile."

He motioned with his head towards the right from where the smoke was rising. "Clay furnaces. Mix charcoal and ore equally, throw in furnace. Blow in air with pipes to make fire hot. After long time, draw out iron ingot at bottom."

He pointed to another area where slaves were feverishly using huge hammers on pieces of glowing iron. "Hammer to get rid of impurities. Make cleaner iron", he whispered.

"Cai, we are not here to learn how to make iron. We are here to take the iron", Hostilius interjected. "Knowledge better weapon than sword", was Cai's only retort.

"There are at least two centuries of legionaries guarding the slaves", Gordas said. "Another two centuries man the palisade at the entrance." He motioned with his head toward the sheer cliffs created by the mining all around. "No one is getting in that way."

"So, what's your clever plan Domitius?" Hostilius asked when we were walking back to our horses.

"We charge the palisade and overwhelm them with sheer numbers", I said.

It didn't sound clever, but it appealed to Gordas.

"Great plan, Eochar. Best you had in some time", he said and slapped my back. That's Huns for you.

Chapter 24 – Strigoi

Although well-guarded, the mine was a soft target.

The assault was all but spectacular. The barbarians charged the wooden palisade, releasing hundreds of arrows as they approached. The legionaries had little choice but to hide behind their shields. When the Huns were alongside the wall, they simply stood on the backs of their horses, which by the way, every Hun could do with his eyes closed, grabbed the top of the logs and hauled themselves onto the rampart. Within heartbeats the barbarians had secured the wall and the gates were open.

Hostilius, Cai and I did not participate in the assault, but the Hun commander relished it.

The gates to the compound opened from the inside. Gordas was first to exit. He had sustained a bloody nose in the fight, and consequently blood was dripping down his chin. He walked over to me to collect his horse which I was holding for him.

He smiled, revealing bloodstained teeth, a result of his nosebleed. "The Romans fought well. The centurion knows how to use his shield", he said and gestured to his injured face.

I started to speak, but the Hun held up his hand. "I know what you will ask, Eochar. Yes, we have bound the ones who are not with Tengri. They fought bravely and will be spared." He shook his head. "You truly are a strange one."

I entered the gate and took in the scene.

Down in the pit, the Huns were rounding up the hundreds of slaves. To the one side, the legionaries had formed a testudo formation and the Huns were picking them off one by one as gaps appeared between the shields.

Hostilius scowled, dismounted, and approached the one-sided battle with Gordas walking at his side. The Hun motioned to his warriors to cease their assault.

Hostillius yelled. "Who commands? Show yourself centurion", using his parade ground Primus Pilus voice. A Roman reluctantly stepped forward from the men who had by then grounded their shields.

He addressed Hostilius: "Who are you, Roman traitor?"

I was watching intently now, as I knew that the words of the centurion would not sit well with my friend.

"I am Primus Pilus Hostilius Proculus, IV Italica. Loyal to the murdered emperor, Gordian III."

His hand went to his sword. "Do you support the usurper and murderer, Phillip the Arab?" he growled.

The centurion realised that Hostilius was no imposter. Gone was the defiant attitude. He came to attention, saluted, and stared straight ahead, not making eye contact.

"I take orders, Primus Pilus", he said.

"Good, then. I give orders. Tell your men to lay down their weapons and armour. Then march to the slave barracks. Choose wisely, and you might live."

Before long the legionaries, now stripped to their tunics, were frog-marched to the slave barracks and the door barred from the outside.

I turned my attention to the slaves. "Gordas, have your men escort them to the gate and release them."

We had no use for slaves, as it was important for the army to remain mobile.

Gordas walked towards the slaves, unaware of his terrifying appearance, exacerbated by the dried blood that stained his mouth. They recoiled at his approach, causing the Hun to snarl and appear even more vicious. His hand went to his sword.

I heard terrified voices speaking in local Latin rise above the murmurs. "It is the Strigoi, come to drink our blood" and "Look, he has feasted on the blood of the Romans already."

To be fair, Gordas did resemble the undead monster from the local tales, even without his bloody mouth.

191

I intervened. "Come, you are free to go", I said. "Follow me to the gate."

They flowed around a scowling Gordas like water avoids a boulder in a stream. Soon they were running away from the palisade, to freedom. Unbeknown to me, this act of kindness probably saved our lives.

It took some time to load the hundreds of iron ingots onto the spare horses. The ingots weighed around thirty-five pounds each, which allowed a horse to carry two. The challenging part was to secure the load properly.

Within less than a watch since we had first arrived, we exited the main gate, heading back to the camp of the Roxolani.

We had travelled less than half a mile when slaves came running down the hillsides of the narrow valley that allowed access to the mine.

I rode up to an old slave. "Who is out there, slave?" I asked.

"Great horse lord, please have mercy. The forest is crawling with Roman legionaries. They have killed many, but we were too slow to run away from the Strigoi. The Romans did not see us."

"Back to the mine", I yelled, realising an ambush was upon us. We turned our horses and galloped back to the safety of the palisade, while hundreds of legionaries, in tight ranks, streamed down the slopes of the hill. More were exiting the forest.

I cursed myself under my breath. My eagerness to gain loot, coupled with my hubris, had lulled me into the belief that the Romans were fooled. My scouts should have reconnoitred the forest as well as our road home.

We closed the gate and barred it from the inside. Half of the Huns lined the palisade, each holding a strung bow with a full quiver slung over the shoulder. The warriors defending the palisade had reluctantly taken up legionary shields, placing it at their feet in case of need.

My emotions must have been written on my face. Cai placed his hand on my shoulder. "Lucius of Da Qin. Wise man of Serica once said 'mistake not exist, only lesson'. Put from mind. Learn." He tapped his index finger against his temple.

Hostilius interjected. "Looks to be two cohorts. It's not the emblem of the XIII Gemina or the V Macedonica, Domitius." He squinted. "Let me go get a prisoner."

We watched the cohorts form up four hundred paces from the palisade while Hostilius went about his business. He eventually reappeared with the captured centurion in tow.

"Tell the tribune", Hostilius instructed the man.

"Tribune", he said and saluted. "Word is that General Quintus Decius was sent from Sirmium to rid us of the barbarians." He looked around nervously, his gaze alternating between Gordas and myself.

"Tell me about Decius", I said

"Don't know much about him, sir. Other than… never mind sir, just army talk."

I scowled.

"They call him the arse-licker of the emperor, sir", he said and swallowed nervously.

I nodded. I have heard the name before. Like me, Gaius Quintus Decius hailed from Sirmium. My father, Nik, had mentioned his name from time to time. A firm supporter of Philip the Arab. Clever, devious and heartless. He was not to be underestimated.

"Which legions are under his command?"

"Not sure, sir, but some say the VII Claudia and … ", he suddenly went quiet.

"And?" Hostilius barked. "Speak up, man."

The centurion swallowed, fearing the ire of Hostilius. "And the IV Italica, sir."

Chapter 25 – Decius

"At least", Hostilius sighed and motioned with his head towards the assembled cohorts, "it is not the IV Italica drawn up against us."

Hostilius knew the ways of the legions. "They won't attack today. For now they are just intimidating us, playing with our minds", he said.

I must have frowned. "Look Domitius, no waterskins. Only bloody idiots go into a battle without water. I'd wager they aren't idiots, eh?"

He tapped his ear with his finger. "Listen. Hear the faint noises? They are digging a trench across the valley floor where it is narrowest, I estimate only sixty paces across. Even the Urugundi won't break a line thirty men deep. They will leave a piece intact, maybe ten paces, but that won't help us 'cause that's where they will build a gate of sorts."

I nodded, accepting the truth of his words.

"What do you advise?" I asked.

"Get some sleep", he said. "I will arrange for Gordas to rotate the men on the walls in four shift cycles. Then I will join you." As I walked off he added: "And pray the war god gives you a plan."

* * *

The stalemate lasted three days.

Late afternoon on the third day Cai called me to the wall. Hostilius and Gordas were waiting for us.

The Primus Pilus pointed to the distant valley entrance. "They were waiting on reinforcements. Judging by the standards, I guess it's another cohort. They will attack soon. Mark my words."

Early the following morning I woke to a familiar sound. A Roman buccina called the legionaries to assemble. They would attack with the rising sun behind them. Their commander was no fool.

I had no grand plan, apart from one surprise. We had stacked the heavy iron ingots on the inside of the walkway and assigned warriors to the task of throwing them over the wall where the Romans would attack.

Before long the cohorts were drawn up in battle formation. The frontage of the wall measured one hundred paces, which worked in our favour, as the Romans could only bring so many of their men to bear.

The cohorts advanced. I noticed legionaries carrying crude ladders that they would use to scale the twelve-foot palisade.

I passed the word along the line. "Concentrate your arrows on the men carrying the ladders. They will find it difficult to use their shields."

At two hundred and fifty paces the buccina announced the testudo formation. As one the rear ranks raised their shields to protect against missiles from above. Even though I harboured ill feelings towards the emperor, the legions never failed to impress with their discipline.

The Huns released well-aimed arrows with very little success. The Roman advance continued as they shuffled closer and closer to the palisade. Every few heartbeats a cry emanated from the enemy ranks when an arrow flew true.

But their advance was inexorable.

Hostilius said to Gordas: "The first four ranks will throw their pila when they are twenty paces from the palisade. Warn the warriors. As soon as the Romans expose themselves, loose as many arrows into their ranks as possible, then duck!" He added: "Do not use the shields. The spears will render them useless. Save the shields for when they scale the wall."

When the command came, the Huns were ready. At least a hundred legionaries fell to the barbarian arrows. Only a

197

handful of Gordas's warriors were too slow to evade the Roman spears.

The legionaries moved forward and the first of the heavy ladders crashed against the palisade.

When fighting from horseback, the Huns knew no equal. The warriors were well-armed and armoured, but the armour was designed to repel arrows, not sword strikes. The Romans, to the contrary, were trained for close quarter combat. They were ideally equipped for the task at hand.

I afforded a peek down the line and took in the snarling Huns. Their tattooed and scarred faces gleamed with sweat, the muscles rippling on their arms.

It would be close - the animal-like ferocity of the Huns pitched against the discipline of the men in red.

A ladder was raised right in front of us. I had to take a small step back when it thudded against the top of the wooden palisade. A legionary shield appeared at the top of the ladder. I tried to strike overhand, at his head, but the glancing blow slid off his helmet. A gladius snaked out from behind the shield and I blocked the strike with my own scutum.

Hostilius broke the stalemate. He grabbed an iron ingot and rammed it overhead into the shield of the unfortunate soldier.

The Roman's shield shattered and he fell over backwards, the ingot clearing the ladder of men all the way down.

The Primus Pilus grabbed another ingot while I covered his body with my shield, and hurled it into the men massing beneath the wall. "This is your payment for murdering the emperor. Bloody bastards!" he shouted in his centurion's voice.

As Hostilius bellowed, I noticed the legionaries pause for a moment in time. The confidence carried in the voice of a commanding officer can be a powerful thing.

All along the wall, ingots were thrown into the ranks down below, with a devastating effect. No Roman shield can protect against a thirty-five pound ingot lofted from a twelve foot wall.

Efficiently the Roman dead and wounded were dragged to the rear of the line. Fresh ranks of legionaries moved to the front, seamlessly continuing the assault.

Along the palisade, attackers were gaining a foothold. The Huns fought back ferociously, but the shields and armour of the legionaries were superior, their short stabbing swords ideal for this manner of warfare.

The Romans had another surprise in store. Another shield appeared at the top of the ladder as the buccina issued a command. The legionary ascending the ladder paused. A volley of auxiliary arrows struck the defenders on the wall. Many of them toppled backwards, allowing more Romans onto the rampart.

I managed to dispatch the legionary on the ladder with a thrust of my gladius. Hostilius turned to me, wide-eyed. I was convinced that he had been wounded, as I had never seen him react that way. He yelled something to Cai and Gordas, which I was unable to discern above the din of the battle.

Then I felt a dampness where my neck met my shoulder. My arm went numb, the blade dropping from my grip. Centurions shouted, buccinas issued commands, Huns howled and the earth started to vibrate. My vision blurred and I had the sense that I was floating, suddenly unconcerned. Cai caught me before I could plunge to my death.

Chapter 26 – Pledge

The world slowly shifted back into focus. Marcus's smiling face gave me the reassurance that I was still on this side of the River Styx.

He turned his head towards the entrance. "He's awake!" he shouted. Within heartbeats Gordas, Hostilius and Bradakos all bunched into the tent.

I noticed Cai sitting cross-legged on the other side of my bed. He held a small cup in his hand and I knew what was coming. "Drink this, Lucius of Da Qin", he ordered. I swallowed the thick, vile liquid. "Good. Powdered sea-horse mixed with blood of goat. Get better quick." I was ready to vomit.

Cai grinned. "Only joke. Herb mixed with honey."

"Good thing wear yellow silk. Arrow go in here." He placed his finger where his neck met his shoulder. "Small thread of many silk layer trap iron head." He held up the bloodstained silk undergarment I habitually wore in a fight. "Silk not infect wound like linen", he continued.

Hostilius scowled. "Spare us the wonders of Serica, Cai."

"The cohorts of Decius almost kicked our arses, Domitius, but Bradakos arrived just in time. When the Romans realised there were five thousand horse warriors attacking from the rear, they ran for their lives. Half escaped into the forests, half didn't. We burned their corpses three days ago. They fought well and deserved a proper burial."

"Two hundred Huns went to Tengri", Gordas added. He nodded his head slowly in recognition of Hostilius's words. "Next time we will fight them from the saddle. Then we will see."

"We owe you our lives, Bradakos", I said, surprised at the croaking hoarseness of my voice.

Bradakos nodded and said: "Rest now, Eochar. We will feast our victory as soon as you are back on your feet."

I spent the next three days confined to my furs. Cai refused my requests to leave the tent. He repeatedly forced potions down my throat and dressed my wound twice a day, applying herb pastes and honey.

Vibius, Marcus and Bradakos visited regularly and relayed the happenings, which I pieced together afterwards.

* * *

While I was leading the raid on the iron mine, Marcus was doing the same to the north. He led a thousand Roxolani in a raid on the salt mine at Potaissa. The raid was successful and the warriors returned with spare horses loaded with the scarce commodity. The cohorts of the V Macedonica stationed at the fort of Potaissa did not offer battle, but remained within the safety of the walls.

On their return to the Roxolani camp near Apulum, they found that we had failed to return from our raid on the iron mine at Deva. Bradakos did not tarry, and sent out scouts immediately.

They returned with news of two legions travelling north, via the Mures River valley, heading for Apulum. There, Bradakos and his eight thousand Roxolani, with Marcus's assistance, ambushed the Romans. They cleverly annihilated the exploratores and caught the legions in a broad section of the valley. The horse warriors surprised the Roman army while they were spread out on the march. Although they did not inflict heavy casualties, Decius and his men retreated to the fort at Apulum in disorganised mobs.

Having removed the threat, the Roxolani found the three cohorts that besieged the mine. On the advice of Marcus, they waited until the legions commenced their attack before falling on the rear of the Romans, who had left none to guard the ditch.

With enemies on both sides, and greatly outnumbered, the cohorts scattered before the Scythians.

* * *

On the morning of the fourth day after I had regained consciousness, frustration overcame me. A scowling Cai allowed me to walk around outside. "Should rest one day more. Tonight wound bleed again."

Fortunately, Cai's prediction did not materialise. After the sun set we arrived at the tent of the king to attend a feast in celebration of our recent victory. Rather than the raucous barbarian celebration I expected, it resembled an intimate family gathering.

Cai and I joined Marcus, Vibius, Hostilius and Gordas in the king's tent. Pezhman, now serving as a warrior and scout of the Roxolani, was still in awe of Bradakos and preferred to spend time with his barbarian friends.

I invited him, but he declined. "I am at long last accepted by the horse warriors, Prince Eochar", he said. "Should I dine with the king, they will push me to the side. They will be jealous."

The Roxolani had looted the baggage train of Legate Quintus Decius, with the best pickings ending up on the king's table.

We dined on succulent cuts of beef, aromatic mutton laced with spices, and exotic fruit, all washed down with the best red I have had in months.

"There is an issue that I wish to discuss", Bradakos said once we had our fill.

"The legions of Decius will surely be blocking our route home, to the north. We have surprised the legions once. We will not be so fortunate next time."

Arash whispered into my ear. "Then we must leave at first light", I said.

"I agree", Hostilius said, slapping his thigh with his open hand. "We should attack immediately."

I smiled. "No centurion, we will ride south and strike into the heart of Moesia."

"We were told that Decius was appointed as imperial legate of the Danubian legions some time ago. He would therefore be stationed at Viminacium. The VII Claudia mans the forts along the southern bank of the Danube between their home base of Viminacium and Ratiara farther east, which is a stretch of more than a hundred and thirty miles."

Marcus grinned then. "You are truly a crafty bastard", he said. "Decius must have collected most of the VII Claudia before crossing the river at Drobetae with the help of the Danubian fleet."

I nodded, unrolling the Roman itinerarium. "He would then have moved north through the Iron Gates, Ad Medium and the Porta Orientalis pass." I pressed my finger on the document. "Here at Tibiscum, he turned east and moved along the Bistra River Valley until he reached Ulpia Traiana, which is less than a day's ride south of us."

"And the Danubian limes will be poorly garrisoned", Hostilius added. "Most of the legions have been sent against the Goths. What was left was taken by Decius."

I savoured the last mouthful of the red. "We follow the same route as Decius, only we will move faster. When we reach the Danube we will move east and join my brother-in-law."

Bradakos smiled. "It is decided. I agree." He slapped my back, causing me to flinch with pain.

The king did not apologize. "The wound will make you stronger, brother", he said.

"There is one last thing, Bradakos", I said. "Draw your blade."

My mentor and friend looked confused for a moment, then his expression turned serious.

"It is not necessary, Eochar."

"It is", I said.

He drew his magnificent blade, which once belonged to my uncle Apsikal, and placed it on his lap.

Hostilius, Gordas and I had discussed this and as one we stood. We kneeled in front of Bradakos, simultaneously placing our hands on the sword.

"A gift of a life demands the pledge of a life. Eochar of the Roxolani makes this pledge freely, witnessed by the god of war and fire."

Gordas and Hostilius followed suit.

Chapter 27 – The Iron Gates (July 245 AD)

"Why do they call it the 'Iron Gates'?" Vibius asked.

Marcus had the answer. "Iron is scarce on the Sea of Grass, but plentiful in Transsilvania. For many generations the Scythians, Thracians and other tribes traded with the Dacians for iron. Even Rome bought iron from here. Most of the metal was brought via this route into Scythia, hence the name the 'Iron Gates'."

"Until Traianus decided he wanted the iron for himself", Bradakos sneered. "From then, Rome cut off our supply of iron. But two thousand iron ingots is a fine gesture of reparation."

We had been on the road for four days, our spare horses heavily laden with iron and salt, which slowed our progress.

An advance scout returned, reining in next to the king. "There is a Roman town up ahead, lord. The people have fled, lord. It is the same as everywhere else."

It came as no surprise that the townspeople and garrisons of the small forts had fled before the advance of the Scythians. A single century was no match for eight thousand horse warriors.

Marcus and Vibius joined the scouts to investigate. My wound still troubled me so I remained with the vanguard of the army.

In any event, we soon arrived at the deserted town. The Romans had cleared much of the forest, which allowed the army sufficient space to set up camp next to the river. We had hardly settled in when Vibius and Marcus returned.

"Better come with us", Marcus said, wearing a serious expression.

Bradakos, Cai and I mounted, with Marcus and Vibius leading the way. We travelled for nearly three miles on a decent road, rounding a forested hill. We rode south, turned east, then north again.

I was concerned that some wayward warriors had committed unimaginable atrocities, but was surprised when a grinning Marcus led us to a Roman building surrounded by lush fig orchards.

Recognition dawned on me. I turned to Bradakos. "Allow us to show you some Roman hospitality", I said, and dismounted next to the imposing stone and brick structure.

Before long, we were all relaxing in the warm water of the Roman baths, fed by the natural hot springs flowing from the rock. The walls of the complex were richly decorated with mosaics depicting Hercules. An inscription explained that in days of old, a weary Hercules bathed in the water of the springs.

For Bradakos it was a new experience. He wondered at the artwork and workmanship of the Roman builders. "So, this is what you call civilisation?" he asked.

"Yes", I said.

"It is truly as if the gods had built it", he said. "I fear that these things", he gestured to all that surrounded us, "will make a hard warrior as soft as a merchant."

"It will, brother. It surely will", I said, and immersed myself in the warm water.

* * *

We arrived on the northern bank of the Great River two days later.

Gordas and Bradakos stared at the southern bank, more than half a mile distant.

"There used to be a bridge here", Marcus said, and pointed to stone pillars dotting the surface of the river in a straight line.

Gordas shook his head. "It is not possible. How are men able to build in water?"

"The legions cut a channel upriver and redirected the water farther downstream. The bridge was nearly a mile long, fifty feet wide and the road surface sixty feet above the water."

Gordas smirked. "If what you say is true, Roman, where is it then?"

I interjected. "Gordas, the Romans burned their own bridge a hundred years ago to keep out the likes of the Roxolani and the Urugundi."

He grinned like a wolf. "The Urugundi do not need a bridge to cross the Mother River. All we need is winter, then Tengri gives us a bridge."

He was right, of course.

For days we travelled east, following the northern bank of the Danube while staying out of sight of the Roman sentries on the southern bank. The horde raided the vulnerable local villages and even resorted to trading with the Romanised folk in the larger settlements protected by higher walls. War is never a barrier for men to profit.

Bradakos sent out groups of scouts, but they all told the same tale: The limes to the east was deserted. Only the larger towns with high walls were garrisoned.

It took the best part of a moon to plunder our way east across the Dacian countryside.

Eventually we arrived at the Rabon River. We camped on the western bank, close to where its waters flowed into the Danube.

Here the islands and sandbanks, combined with the slow current, created an ideal location for barbarians like us to cross the river.

The Romans had wisely built a fort on the southern bank of the Great River. This fort, integrated into the Danubian limes, was called Augustae. It was built to monitor this section of the river, which is fordable during late summer when the water level is low.

Bradakos called a council.

"Our saddlebags are bulging with gold. We have taken herds of sheep and goats. The spare horses struggle under a heavy burden of iron and salt." He took a swig of looted wine. "But, while we are unopposed, why should we return home?"

"The army of Decius would surely have followed us south through the Iron Gates. They are either somewhere west of us, or they might have crossed the Danube into Moesia", Marcus said. "Philip the Arab will not sit idly by while we ravage the Empire. If he does not mobilise the legions, he will lose the confidence of the legates, which will not end well for him."

"Whatever we decide", I said, "will be a disaster if we forfeit the plunder. I say we send the loot home in wagons that we can, er… procure in Dacia, east of the Rabon. If we are unable to move fast, we are vulnerable."

Hostilius nodded. "Our speed is a great strength. Send the loot home, it will make us strong again."

"I agree", Vibius said. "Out of curiosity, has anyone received news of Tarbus and the Carpiani?"

Bradakos sighed. "The path of the Roxolani has separated from that of the Carpiani. I am not concerned with the actions of Tarbus."

It took a moon for the army to gather enough wagons along with the inevitable additional loot.

A thousand Roxolani and two hundred of Gordas's warriors accompanied the heavily laden wagons and livestock that travelled north and east, towards the heartland of the tribe.

Bradakos, Hostilius and I watched as the last of the wagons struggled across the Rabon. "I have sent scouts across the Danube, and they have returned. The limes south of the river is in disarray and weakly garrisoned. We will be able to breach with ease."

"Do you recall the centurion at the iron mine, Domitius?" Hostilius asked.

I nodded. "Whatever happened to him and his men?"

"We left them at the mine", he answered.

He noticed my enquiring stare. "Alive", he added.

"Anyway", he continued, "I shared an amphora or two of wine with him. Told me interesting things. He said that the Arab has raised taxes throughout the Empire. Half the gold will be used to pay the Persians. The other half of the gold he is spending to upgrade Trimontium, where he was born. Even changed the name to Philippopolis. He has ordered the building of arenas, theatres, aqueducts and the like. Apparently he's erecting statues of himself and Priscus all over the place." He reflected for a moment. "Pity he and his brother are as ugly as shit. The statues have probably ruined the whole bloody place."

"Nonetheless, Philippopolis is overflowing with gold and the walls are not done yet. Maybe we should pay them a visit?"

I speculated. "The area is probably crawling with legionaries."

"You see, Domitius, that's just the thing. Apparently there are no legions in the vicinity of the city. Or that's what I was told. Chances are we'll ride from here to the gates of Philippopolis without laying eyes on a legionary."

He was very wrong, of course, but not in the way that anyone could have expected.

Chapter 28 – IV Italica

Two days later the mobile, albeit less numerous Scythian army, crossed the Danube unchallenged, entering the Roman province of Moesia Inferior.

We rode at the head of an army of seven thousand horse warriors. Five hundred of Gordas's Urugundi remained, the rest were Roxolani.

Unlike when we were in Dacia, we did not need an itinerarium. Marcus, Hostilius, Vibius and I had travelled through Moesia a few years earlier when we camped outside of Philippopolis with the barbarian foederati during Gordian III's eastern campaign.

"We need to make our way east", Hostilius said. "A major road connects Oescus on the Danube with Philippopolis in Thracia. This road runs straight from north to south. It's as if Fortuna is levelling the way." This, of course, would soon prove not be the case.

In any event, we travelled east, based on the sound advice of the Primus Pilus. The warriors did not raid other than to put an arrow into a wayward sheep or a lost goat. We rode with a purpose. Revenge. We would plunder the favourite city of the man who had betrayed us. Although the emperor was not within our reach, we would destroy that which was dear to him, and gain much gold in the process.

That was what we thought until a confused-looking scout arrived on a lathered horse.

He reined in and inclined his head, addressing the king. "Lord, there are men on the road."

Bradakos scowled. "Are they merchants? Maybe soldiers?"

"Lord, I do not know. Many men are on the road. Thousands. They are dressed like Roman warriors, lord."

Bradakos turned to us. "Primus Pilus Hostilius, it seems your information was wrong."

"Lord", the scout started again, "it must be Roman warriors, lord, but it is not the legion."

The king, now clearly irritated, dismissed the scout with a wave of his hand.

"What do you make of this, Eochar?" he said.

"Let us see with our own eyes", I said.

My companions and I joined the king and we rode to see for ourselves. We formed the vanguard with the guards of the king trailing close behind. It was open country filled with fields and orchards. We did not fear an ambush.

Soon our path intersected the main road to Philippopolis.

The scout was still with us. "They are on this road, lord. We will see them before we reach the third stone on the side of the road."

I gathered from the scout's words that the strange men were close.

We cantered down the road until we noticed a group of men approaching in the distance.

We reined in five hundred paces from the mob, coming to a complete stop on the crest of a low hill.

"They are dressed as legionaries", Hostilius said, "but they do not march as legionaries."

He looked left, right and behind him. "Smells like a bloody trap, but I can see for miles. Don't understand it."

I turned to Bradakos. "Allow us to go speak with them."

He nodded. Hostilius, Marcus and Gordas followed me.

"You will scare them, my friend", I said to Gordas. "I will call you if I wish to scare them."

Gordas turned his horse and placed an arrow on the string. "It is only three hundred paces, Eochar. Just raise your arm and they die."

Remembering Gordas's boast, we stopped three hundred paces from where Bradakos and his guards were waiting.

The mob of men had also come to a stop. They were legionaries without a doubt, yet they did not march in ranks, nor did they display standards.

A group of three men detached from the mob and slowly made their way down the road in our direction.

When they were fifty paces distant, a wide grin split Hostilius's bearded face. For a moment I was confused, but then I recognized one of the men, dressed as a centurion. It was Didius Castus, my stuttering optio from years earlier, who had risen through the ranks to lead the seventh cohort.

The other two were both senior centurions, namely Statius Timoni, who used to be in charge of the second cohort and Cassio Rufinus, whose unit had slipped my mind.

"You'd better not be wasting my bloody time or I will have you all on latrine duty for the rest of your short, miserable lives!" Hostilius boomed in his parade ground voice when the men were twenty paces from us.

A few things happened almost simultaneously.

The three men came to an abrupt halt, with Didius coming to attention, and his comrades staring at us in wonder, their mouths slightly ajar.

218

It took a few heartbeats for the baffled men to regain their composure. My former optio awkwardly stood at ease when he realised his mistake.

Didius squinted into the light. "Umbra? P…Primus Pilus? Is it really you? Are you an apparition sent by the gods to punish us for what we have done?"

I walked towards him and clasped his arm. "No my friend, it is far worse than you have imagined. We are not the tools of the gods, we are the vanguard of the Goths."

They wanted to protest, but I held up my hand. "Go tell the men to stay where they are. They will be in grave danger if they travel farther on this road. When you return we will join Primus Pilus Hostilius and Tribune Marcus. We need to hear your tale."

Bradakos and his entourage rode back to the Scythian army with a reluctant Gordas in tow. The Roxolani would not advance until we understood the situation.

On the return of the centurions, we walked to the distant treeline where the road crossed the Utus River. I took two wineskins from my saddle. We all sat down in the shade of a great oak on the bank of the stream.

We had known each other for years and all felt at ease. I passed the wineskin around and everyone drank deeply.

Then Didius told his tale.

"Tribune Umbra, we heard that you, the Primus Pilus and Tribune Marcus were exiled for cowardice and insubordination. They told us you tried to kill the emperor and that you were executed."

"We didn't believe a word of it, sir, 'cause if you had really tried to kill him he wouldn't be alive, would he?" He grinned and continued. "But we were told you were dead so we just carried on. We had no choice, sir."

He accepted the wineskin, drank and passed it on. "The legate and the tribunes were recalled soon after, and they sent us brand-new ones fresh from Rome. Never been in the sun, all white as snow. Knew nothing 'bout fighting either."

"When did Senator Decius arrive, Centurion?" Marcus asked.

"They sent him soon after we heard that the barbarians had invaded Dacia. We heard horror stories about them barbarians ripping the limbs from the officers."

He looked over his shoulder as if expecting a barbarian to materialise.

"The IV Italica marched immediately and the VII Claudia joined us along the way, sir."

"They marched us at double pace, all the way up the Iron Gates until some men collapsed. They're good boys, sir, same as you remember, but the officers were all mounted and they didn't see it our way."

"Old Tertius from the first of the second was flogged to death, sir, 'cause he couldn't keep up."

I noticed Hostilius's face turn red with rage. His hand went to the hilt of his gladius.

"Long ago Tertius saved my life", Hostilius growled. "Give me a name."

Didius averted his gaze, and looked down at the ground. "Senator Decius made us watch, sir. One of them speculatores used the scourge on him. Don't know his name, sir."

"Then the horse barbarians attacked us out of nowhere, sir. We didn't even have our shields uncovered. Some of the boys couldn't get their helmets on. It was a bloody mess, sir."

"I told the tribune earlier that we should march in full gear, like Tribune Umbra always had us do, but he laughed at me. Called me a coward in my face. Afterwards he told a different story. Said I didn't follow his orders."

"The men haven't been paid for a while as well, sir. It's not like it was in the days when the boy Gordian was emperor."

"Bloody bastard is giving all your coin to the Sasanians, that's why you haven't been paid", Hositlius interjected.

221

"The boys refused to march any farther, sir. In fact, we all refused. Legate Decius became very angry. He had us assemble on the parade ground. Told us we were a disgrace and that we failed him by allowing the barbarians to kick our arses."

"He discharged us then for cowardice, sir. You don't get any pension if you get discharged disgracefully, you know."

I couldn't help but wonder whether the reason for the discharge was the inability of the treasury to pay the legion.

"So why are you here, travelling north? "Should you not be heading south, to Philippopolis?" I asked.

Didius stared at me as if I had asked him why the sky was blue.

"Been there already, Tribune Umbra. We went to talk with the emperor, to ask him for our coin. We wanted to ask him to set right the mess of Senator Decius."

He sighed. "Emperor chased us away like dogs, sir. Threatened to set the legions on us."

"But he is in Rome, isn't he?" Marcus asked.

"With respect, sir, the emperor arrived in Philippopolis about a moon ago. He's got three legions with him, sir. He's here to chase the barbarians back across the Danube."

It was his turn to take another swallow. "We are desperate, sir. We got no food, in fact, apart from our swords and shields, we got nothing. Most of us have nowhere to go, the killing business is all we are good at. It's all we know."

I am not a man prone to pity, but in that moment I experienced deep sympathy for the men sitting across from me. I met Hostilius's gaze and I saw the same emotion in his eyes.

Marcus put it into words. "Lucius, the same monster who murdered your father wronged these men. I know many of them. It feels as if they are my family. We have a duty to come to the aid of our brothers."

He was not ashamed to say it out loud.

I watched the reaction of the three centurions. In that moment they would have followed him into the depths of Hades.

Looking back, that was the moment in which, I believe, the seed was planted in the minds of the men of the Danubian legions. The idea that Marcus Aurelius Claudius deeply cared about their fate. He was already known as a capable military man, but in the end, to achieve greatness, so much more than mere competency is required.

Chapter 29 - Orator

Early the following morning, Marcus and I sat in the tent of my mentor. Hostilius did not join us as he had 'some matters to attend to', to use his own words

The king listened intently, amazed at our retelling of the story of the IV Italica.

"Bradakos, these men are warriors. Arguably the best legion in the whole of Roman lands. They deserve better", I said.

He said nothing for a while, deep in thought.

Then the king of the Roxolani stood. "Go now, Prince Eochar. You have my blessing. Recruit the IV Italica to fight with the tribe. I know that it is what you wish for." We turned to leave, but he added: "We will pay them the gold that they are owed by the oathbreaker. The gold which we have taken from the lands of Rome."

Before we could leave, a scout arrived to report to the king.

"Lord, a Roman legion is marching north, along the Roman road. They are heading for the men Lord Eochar spoke with yesterday. They will reach them within a watch, lord."

Bradakos grinned. "Take Gordas and his men, Eochar. Send a message if you are in need of the Roxolani."

We rode to inform Hostilius of the king's decision, finding the Primus Pilus clean-shaven and immaculately kitted out in full Roman uniform.

I narrowed my eyes. "Primus Pilus, were you forewarned about the king's decision or have you recently been blessed with the sight?"

Hostilius was all business. "Tribune, I did some thinking during the night. My place is with my legion. The gods have sent my brothers to me."

I shared with him the words of the king.

Less than a third of a watch had passed when we arrived at the campsite of the men of the IV Italica.

They had no senior officers to guide them. They were leaderless, without morale, their dignity taken away from them. That is until Hostilius arrived.

I watched as he rounded up the centurions and expertly put them to work. Soon the whole mob of legionaries assembled to hear his words.

"Why are you here?" Hostilius barked.

The Primus Pilus was not only well-respected, he was widely feared.

Silence descended on the ranks as none of the legionaries wished to be singled out as the target of Hostilius's ire.

The centurion knew all by name and he lifted his vine cane, pointing at a legionary in the front of the mob. The Primus Pilus growled: "Publius Urvinus, third century, fourth cohort. Why are you here?"

Publius looked around nervously, but there was no way out of his predicament. "We are in the legions to defend Rome against them barbarians, sir."

Hostilius pointed to a second victim. "Marcus Furius, fifth century, second cohort. Why are you here?"

Marcus tried not to make eye contact, but after a moment he said: "We must honour our soldier's oath to the emperor, sir. Shouldn't we?"

Hostilius continued, now in his booming Primus Pilus voice. "Let me tell you whoresons why I joined the legions. I did it for the gold and the loot."

"All else is shit. Isn't it?"

A grumbling of agreement could be heard from within the massed ranks of the soldiers.

"Did you go to Philippopolis to ask the emperor to kill barbarians? Did you ask him whether you could honour your oath? Bloody-well no!"

"You walked all this way to ask the bastard to give you the coin due to you."

I could hear a few "yes, centurion" calls coming from the ranks.

He pointed to me and Marcus, a few paces away. "Tribune Marcus and Tribune Umbra have arranged that you will receive all the gold that you are due!"

A deafening roar went up from the ranks, but Hostilius roared: "Silence!"

"Who saved your miserable lives at Rhesaina? Was it the emperor?"

"No. It was Tribune Umbra and them Goths", the mob responded as one.

Hostilius was not done yet. "As we speak, a legion is marching against you. They will be here in less than a third of a watch. The emperor has sent them to kill you. You have been betrayed."

Shouts of anger could be heard, echoing through the ranks.

The Primus Pilus pointed to the five hundred Hun riders milling about in the distance.

"We have a chance to regain our honour. We will join the Goths, and by doing so, we will repay them the debt of honour.

227

We will avenge the murder of the true emperor. We will show the usurper-emperor why the IV Italica is known as the best there is."

"What say you?"

The mob roared their approval.

Hostilius took these broken men and gave them a modicum of dignity, and a chance to regain their honour. More importantly, he would give them gold.

He walked over to us and said in a low voice: "Domitius, now it's your turn. You bloody better have a plan."

I smiled. "I do, Primus Pilus Proculus. But I cannot guarantee that it will be as effective as your speech."

* * *

The IV Italica camped close to the Utus River, north of the wooden Roman bridge. Mayhap camped is the wrong word, as they had no tents but slept in the open, in a disorganized mob.

Hostilius soon took control and restored order. A mile north of the bridge, the IV Italica deployed in battle formation. As I had requested, their frontage was narrow, but many ranks deep.

228

Acting as a screen, the tenth cohort was deployed between the river and the legion. They had their backs to the river, walking slowly towards the ordered ranks of their comrades. This would create the scenario the approaching legion expected to encounter. A mob of leaderless, hungry, demoralized men that would offer no resistance.

I split the Huns into two equal groups. One I would command, the other group would be led by Gordas. We hid in the dense shrubs and trees that lined the banks of the river.

For the men of the legions it was incomprehensible for the IV Italica to have joined the barbarians. This was the advantage we would exploit.

Before long a Hun scout, who had been watching the bridge, appeared. "Lord, three hundred Roman cavalry approaching the bridge." He wore the look of someone who had more to say. I nodded and he added: "They have fine horses, lord, but they ride poorly. The foot soldiers of the Romans are half a mile behind their horse warriors."

I expected the Roman equestrians to be supremely confident, knowing that they would be attacking foot soldiers without any cavalry support. They would anticipate the mob to scatter in fear of their charge. Therefore I had arranged it to happen exactly in the manner that they expected.

The men of the tenth cohort turned their heads, pointed in the direction of the bridge and started running north along the road. The equestrians waited for all the riders to cross the bridge before they fanned out and advanced in a long line towards the fleeing mob. We remained hidden until the Roman cavalry went from a walk to a canter. The Huns charged from the undergrowth, trailing the equestrians by three hundred paces.

The Roman cavalry spurred their horses to a gallop, riding knee to knee, spears levelled. They were eager to close with the men running for their lives. That is, until the neatly dressed formation of the IV Italica parted briefly to allow their fleeing comrades passage through their ranks. The running mob was replaced by thousands of legionaries in tight ranks, shields grounded.

The Roman riders reined in, halting in confusion. Then they noticed the unidentified horsemen approaching from behind. To his credit, the tribune in command did not panic, but issued orders to dress the line. They levelled their spears and charged at the barbarians who had cut them off from the legion.

But the Urugundi Huns were demons on horseback. Their skill as riders and archers knew no equal. I gave the order and the horde seamlessly spread out in a line to overlap that of the outnumbered Romans. All took three arrows into their draw hands, with their bows in the other. The sturdy Hun horses galloped at full speed, guided only by the thighs of their riders. At a hundred paces, five hundred armour-piercing arrows left the strings with a near flat trajectory. Before the first wave hit, a second flight was in the air, followed by a third in less than a heartbeat.

The equestrians could sooner have ridden into a solid wall. Four out of five Roman horses reached the Huns without their riders, allowing the barbarians to snatch the reins and claim their prizes.

The few Romans who were still in the saddle were either already dead or quickly dispatched with blows from swords or battle-axes. None escaped the slaughter.

The charging horses created a thick dust cloud, masking the battle from the approaching legion. The legionaries loyal to Philip the Arab was chomping at the bit to join the fray and claim their share of the loot, still unaware of what had transpired.

I did not intervene when the Huns looted the dead. I allowed enough time for no more than a quarter of the legion to cross the narrow bridge, then rode closer to the Hun commander.

"Come, Gordas", I shouted. "Summon the warriors, there is more loot to be had."

The two enemy cohorts who had already crossed were assembling two hundred paces from the bridge, on our side of the river. A steady stream of legionaries joined their formation from the rear.

Shouts of surprise rose from the enemy ranks as the barbarian riders emerged from the cloud of dust, walking their horses in the direction of the river. Following in our wake were the dressed ranks of the IV Italica.

The advantage now lay with us, as the cavalry support of the enemy was no more.

When two hundred paces separated us from the enemy legion, Gordas and I peeled from the group and approached the enemy side by side at a slow trot, in the centre of the field. At a hundred paces we diverged as we rode outwards with the intention of returning to the starting point by way of a circular path. Each of us was followed by half of the Hun horde, the warriors riding two abreast.

I slowly increased the pace, going to a canter. The battle fury was building inside my veins, increasing as the pace picked up. A thousand hooves ground the soil to a fine powder that slowly whirled into the air. I nudged Simsek to a gallop, clamped his flanks with my legs and let go of the reins. Then, instinctively, my horn, wood and sinew bow found my left palm. I rode low in the saddle, and reached for three arrows with my right hand while my stallion accelerated.

I knew from experience that the choking dust would have reached the enemy lines. All they would see is a giant cloud, akin to a whirlwind, ascending into the sky. They would not expect what was to come. Never before had they faced the storm.

I straightened the line and emerged from the dust, fifty paces from the front rank of the enemy. I turned my horse with my legs, now riding virtually parallel to the enemy line. The string of the asymmetrical bow was already drawn to my right ear. In that perfect moment when all four of Simsek's legs were in the air I released, aiming at the gap between two legionary shields. As the first arrow struck the shield, I released the second, then the third.

Behind me I heard a sound similar to hail striking a clay roof as hundreds of arrows impacted along a frontage of only twenty paces. I urged Simsek onwards, re-joined the circle, and nocked three arrows as I came around again. This time my second arrow found a minute gap and a legionary fell forward, the arrow embedded in his neck. Armour-piercing war arrows poured through the gap, more legionaries fell, and the screaming intensified. The storm of arrows did not let up. The Roman line was breaking. Then it was my turn again and all three arrows found flesh.

This time I did not turn away, but grabbed my broad-headed spear in one hand and battle-axe in the other. The legionaries to the sides of the gap let down their shields and drew back their pila, then fell backwards, their bodies riddled with arrows. I threw the axe, cleaved a skull and rammed the spear into the shield of another warrior, bowling him over. A legionary stormed forward, sword in hand, but a lasso plucked him off his feet - screaming, he was dragged to his doom.

I yelled a command. The Huns turned their horses and powered away into the dust. Surprisingly retreating on the cusp of victory.

But the joy of the Arab's men were short-lived as the dressed ranks of the IV Italica emerged from the dust, enveloping them from three sides. Attacked from the front and on both flanks, the legionaries retreated across the bridge, many falling to the vengeful blades of their countrymen.

* * *

Later, with darkness falling, I watched the last of the Romans retreat across the bridge. I turned to Gordas. "Burn it."

Before long the flame tongues were reaching high into the sky.

Marcus reined in next to me. "Can't help but think we are burning our bridges", he said.

Chapter 30 – Contubernium

A smiling Gordas was soon showing off the ivory-hilted gladius he had looted from an equestrian tribune. It truly was a fine weapon.

"Tonight I will celebrate with the warriors, Eochar. I know you have friends among the Romans, the men who you shared a tent with many moons ago."

I nodded and set off to find them.

Before long I sat next to a roaring fire among my friends from my old contubernium.

"The lands north of the Danube have been my home for more than a year now, my friends", I said. "What news is there from Rome?"

From experience I knew that gossip was a staple of the rankers.

Ursa smiled. "If information is what you wish for, you've come to the right place, you have."

"We're not the only ones the Arab and his brother are screwing over. Shared a cup with a messenger passing through from Antioch a month or two ago." He took another swig.

Knowing Ursa, I imagined that it was most likely that they shared and amphora, but I just nodded.

"The man told me, in confidence mind you, that Priscus has been given the whole Eastern Empire to rule over. He's raised taxes, he takes bribes, and kills anyone who speaks against him. Sounds like he's as big an arsehole as the Arab."

"I've met him", I said. "He ordered the killing of my family."

The smiles disappeared from their faces and Ursa refilled my cup.

"Tell us", he said. So I did.

"Bloody bastard", Pumilio said when I was done. He eyed me suspiciously. "Why haven't you killed him yet?"

"The time will come, my friend. For now, Arash has other plans."

They all nodded in revered agreement, understanding that the will of the gods must be respected.

"What else is going on in the Empire?" I asked.

"Looks like the peace with the Sasanians the Arab was so proud of is going to shit", Pumilio said.

He took a swallow and continued. "The emperor gave away Armenia to the Sasanians after we had our backsides kicked. Well, Armenia wasn't really his to give, eh? The Parthian families who ruled Armenia for close to two hundred years ignored the wishes of our illustrious emperor and told Shapur and his Sasanians to get the hell out of Armenia. War between Armenia and the Sasanians is a sure thing."

"But the one thing everyone is talking about, is the huge celebrations to be held in less than two years. Rome will be a thousand years old then, and it'll be the biggest party the world has ever seen."

"I've never been to Rome", Ursa said. "Would give anything to be there for the free drink and the beautiful girls. Always had a dream to visit the arena and see them gladiatiors." Little did we know that the gods were listening.

Ursa filled the empty cups again.

He held aloft the substantial wineskin, now half empty. "One of them cavalrymen had this strapped to his saddle." He drank deeply and smacked his lips. "Won't need it where he's going. By the way, I hope Hades is kickin' the shit out of him."

Pumilio chose to disagree. "He was an equestrian, Ursa. I'd wager he had enough gold to make good and proper sacrifices for years. Them equestrians are probably all riding across the Elysian Fields right now."

Pumilio paused to wet his throat.

"Hades ends up havin' his way with the likes of us. Poor soldiers who skimp on sacrifices."

Ursa suddenly appeared worried. He emptied his cup in one gulp and refilled it again. While muttering something, he poured a libation of red wine on the ground.

"Doesn't count if it's looted wine", Pumilio added.

Ursa's hand clutched his amulet. "Don't mind Pumilio, Ursa. He's pulling your leg", I said.

A grinning Pumilio slapped Ursa on the back, causing him to choke and spill his wine.

Silentus cleared his throat. He seldom spoke, but when he did, people listened.

"Umbra, you are still one of us, in here", he tapped his knuckles on his chest, "so I'll say it as it is."

I nodded, not wanting to interrupt.

"The boys in the legion are done with the emperor, sir. Done. We're yours to command. And don't worry overmuch, we're not concerned about taking up arms against Rome. Fact is, we got nothin' against Rome, sir, we just happen to hate and despise this emperor. Maybe we'll get a new one soon. Chances are we'll like him better."

He took a long swig directly from the wineskin, then stared into the fire, as was his habit.

We drank wine and feasted on horsemeat grilled over the coals. It was well after midnight when I eventually retired to my tent. I had overindulged and already regretted it, but the simple logic of my soldier friends put everything in perspective and my mind was at peace.

The sun was high in the sky when Cai kicked my feet. He sniffed the air, scowling. "Smell like place where dog died."

Ignoring the remark, I crawled out of the tent and walked down to the river. A Hun scout was stationed close to the northern bank. "The Romans have retreated south, lord."

I walked upstream a hundred paces and waded into the cool water.

Soon I felt like my old self again. I lay on the riverbank in the soft grass until the sun dried me, then went back to my tent. I took time to comb my hair and beard.

I had neglected to care for my armour after the battle. My eye caught the oiled scale armour, neatly stacked in the corner of my tent. I drew my jian, the blade expertly cleaned and sharpened. All my weapons, including my bow, had been cared for.

Cai was waiting for me when I eventually emerged from my tent.

"Thank you Cai Lun", I said.

"Armour not clean itself" he said. "Not good look like peasant when guests arrive."

I harboured suspicions that Cai was afforded glimpses into the future due to his closeness to the Dao, but he always insisted that it was nothing of the sort. "Just use eyes. Not look with eyes, see with eyes."

All I saw at that moment was Elmanos approaching.

"Lord Eochar, the king requests your company", he said.

Chapter 31 – Goths (September 245 AD)

I accompanied the Roxolani commander to the tent of the king. I was ushered in by a guard, where I came face to face with a grinning Kniva.

He was not only my brother-in-law but also the king, the lawgiver, of the Thervingi Goths.

I went down on one knee, but Ostrogotha, who was also present said: "Rise, Eochar, prince of the Roxolani."

As I came to my feet, Kniva embraced me. "It is good to see you, brother. I hear that you have been busy doing the work of Teiwaz."

I grinned and inclined my head towards the Ostrogothic king, who extended his hand and clasped my arm in a grip of iron.

Bradakos clapped his hands. Soon servants laid on platters of fried smoked pork and prime cuts of mutton roasted over the open fire. Looted amphorae were opened and the rich wine poured into golden goblets.

"Bradakos my friend, I do not see wagons heaped with loot, but I see a Roman legion encamped close by, as if they are your allies. I would that you share your tale with us", Ostrogotha said.

Kniva smiled. "I wager that my sister's husband had a hand in this. I too would hear the tale."

Bradakos held out his oversized goblet. A slave filled it to the brim with red wine, near purple in colour.

He drank deeply. "It will be my pleasure."

My mentor shared the tale of our adventures over the past months. Bradakos viewed me as a younger brother, or even a son. He did not mind heaping praise upon me as he knew that I would never be a threat to his kingship. In fact, his association with me, the messenger of the war god, increased his status in the eyes of his subjects.

Much later, when we had told our story, Ostrogotha spoke.

"You have done well, Bradakos of the Roxolani. Rome is not an easy enemy to contend with." He looked at me sideways. "But I guess it helps to have the messenger of Arash by your side."

I told them then how the IV Italica came to be our allies.

Kniva shook his head in amazement. "A whole Roman legion to fight at our side? If I had not seen it with my own eyes, I would not have believed it."

Slaves refilled our goblets, then Bradakos asked the Gothic kings to tell their tale.

243

"We breached the limes far to the east, at Noviodunum near the Dark Sea. Our warriors overran the Roman fort and put the garrison to the sword. There the armies of the Thervingi and the Gruthungi forded the river and poured across the border into Roman lands."

"Initially we did not encounter any resistance. We raided far and wide, gaining much loot. We scaled the walls of the smaller towns, but did not try to take the well-garrisoned major settlements."

I nodded. "It is wise not to waste the lives of the warriors by storming the high walls of the large towns. More than enough riches is within easy reach."

"You sound just like my son-in-law", Ostrogotha said, and playfully slapped Kniva on the back. It was clear that they had grown close over the past months. I even noticed a hint of pride when the great Gothic king spoke of Kniva's deeds.

Kniva continued: "We slowly worked our way west, stripping the rich countryside of anything of value. It did not take long for the legions to mobilise and regroup. They pursued us, trying to bring us to battle." He grinned then. "But on your advice, brother, we never accepted battle. We scouted well, making sure that we would not be trapped. We, in turn, laid ambushes for the Roman cavalry. Before long they did not venture far from their iron legions. Last we heard was that three Roman legions have congregated near Nicopolis, seventy miles to the east."

"Philip the Arab, the usurper emperor, is but eighty miles south of here with another three legions." I smiled as the Roman strategy became clear to me. "The two Roman armies will advance at the same time. I expect another army is travelling from the west, moving east along the Via Militaris. They wish to trap us within Moesia and kill us all. Your wagons filled with loot will make a fine windfall for the imperial treasury in Rome."

"Then, my friends", Ostrogotha said, "I believe that the time for the Goths and the Roxolani to return home has arrived."

Bradakos sighed. "There is something else."

He took the last swallow from his goblet and a slave hurried over to refill the vessel. "The paths of the Roxolani and the Carpiani have separated."

Ostrogotha frowned, clearly not pleased with the news.

"Tarbus and I see things differently. If we had stayed together, it would not have ended well."

We all knew that the Carpiani answered to the kings of the Goths.

"I will speak to Tarbus", Ostrogotha growled. "I will not have them disrupt the alliance."

His words were also meant as a veiled threat to Bradakos, although the Goths would tread carefully as they feared Octar and his Hun horde.

Bradakos showed his wisdom and said: "I will do all in my power to ensure that the alliance remains."

Satisfied, Ostrogotha nodded. "Bradakos, I have known Tarbus for many seasons. His greed will be his downfall." The king wetted his throat. "But the Carpiani are brave warriors. We cannot allow him to take them down with him. In seasons to come, we will need every warrior we are able to muster. Rome will not forget."

Bradakos raised his goblet and we drank to the success of the alliance.

The Gruthungi king said: "When we are back in our lands, I will meet with the Carpiani king. I will ensure that he stays under the Gothic heel." Little did he know that the next time he would see Tarbus, it would be under less than ideal circumstances.

* * *

The next morning, even before the hundreds of wagons heavy with Roman loot could begin their journey north towards the river, the Scythians left camp.

The Goths escorted the baggage, while the Roxolani, who were by far the better horsemen, scouted the lay of the land. Hostilius and I accompanied Gordas and his remaining half a thousand Urugundi. Vibius was beset by a coughing ailment and Cai insisted that he stayed with the baggage train. Elmanos, who would be scouting south, asked Marcus to accompany them.

We rode north, following the Roman road towards the Danube.

My friends were all capable riders by then. Our tireless Hun steeds enabled us to scout for up to forty miles while still being able to return to camp the same evening.

Our warband was large enough to deter Roman cavalry from engaging us, which allowed us to sacrifice stealth for the benefit of speed.

After a watch of hard riding, we watered the horses in a stream close to the road. Hostilius surveyed the land with an expert eye. "No legion will travel across this terrain. We would do well to stay on the road."

Following the advice of the Primus Pilus, we continued along the Roman road. It was halfway through the second watch of the morning when Gordas pointed to a slight haze on the horizon.

"Men are moving towards us", he said.

I squinted into the distance and noticed the dust typical of a large host on the move.

"Gordas, you truly have eyes like the bird of Tengri", I said. My friend answered with a rare smile. The eagle was not only revered as the bird of the sky god, but was also a symbol of power.

"Let us see who stirs the dust", he said and we kicked our horses to an easy canter.

As we approached, the dust cloud grew in enormity.

Hostilius rode at my side. "That ain't the legions, Domitius. Too much dust for men on foot. Could be they gathered all the mounted auxiliaries this side of Germania, but I doubt it. The auxiliaries are paired with the legions to ensure they behave. If you throw too many of them together you soon end up with an out-of-control barbarian army."

Hostilius, who was riding on my left, put my own thoughts to words. "Could it not be the Carpiani?"

"Speculate is waste of breath. Wait. See with own eyes", came the reply from behind us.

We did not have to wait long.

A group of thirty riders, most probably advance scouts of the approaching column, crested a hill two hundred paces distant. We immediately reined in.

It was too far away to discern their identity. After a few moments two of the riders detached from the group and trotted in our direction, hands held at their sides with open palms facing upwards.

Gordas and I assumed the same pose and rode to meet the unknown riders.

It soon became clear that they were barbarians like us, which did not make it less risky.

Gordas, who was riding on my right, said in a low voice: "I will take the one on the left, he'll be watching you. Make sure you get the one opposite me. Use your axe, it will be the quickest."

Based on his advice, I had no doubt that my Hun friend had previous experience of tribal negotiations.

In any event, extreme measures were not required as a smile split the face of the leader of the approaching men.

"Well met, Lord Eochar", he called out.

I recognized him when he spoke. He was a warrior, oathbound to my friend the Carpiani noble, Thiaper.

"It is good see you, Dardanos. Is all well with your lord?" I replied.

I read the answer on his face before the words were spoken. "He is grievously wounded, lord."

I turned to Dardanos's companion. "Go tell your men to rest." I was a great lord, so he did as he was told.

Gordas may have been a barbarian, but he was extremely perceptive and realised that I needed privacy. "I will order our men to rest, Eochar", he said, turning his horse towards the Urugundi.

"Tell me all, Dardanos", I said and added, "as Arash is your witness."

Chapter 32 – Dardanos

We remained on our horses, halfway between the Carpiani and the Huns. I did not care. Thiaper was a good man, and a friend.

Dardanos told his tale.

"King Tarbus was consumed by rage after we lost so many warriors in our attempt to breach the Roman defences at the Rucar pass, lord."

I nodded as I had witnessed the battle.

"The king blamed King Bradakos of the Roxolani, lord. He said that he had not been forewarned about the artillery of the Romans."

Again I nodded as I was aware of the circumstances surrounding the events.

"Days later, when the Roxolani successfully breached the Roman defences, the Carpiani warriors sang your praises, lord. They said that no one is able to stand against the one who wields the power of Arash. The king became extremely agitated, then ordered us to leave immediately."

Dardanos took a swig from a skin tied to his saddle. "We rode past the Roman fort when king Tarbus ordered lord Thiaper to burn it and nail the Roman warriors to the walls. Lord Thiaper told the king that you had forbidden it. He refused to burn the fort, lord, defying king Tarbus."

"The king called him a coward in front of us all. Tarbus's oathsworn warriors nailed the Romans to the wall and then burned the fort."

He must have seen the unspoken question in my eyes, as he paused to explain. "My lord Thiaper is known as a brave warrior, lord. He has gained a reputation among the tribes of the Carpiani. I think that the king was afraid to order his death. Even some of the king's oathsworn have ties to Lord Thiaper."

Thiaper was a Carpiani noble. Under extreme circumstances, he could challenge the king to combat for the throne. Tarbus knew that ordering my friend's death would most probably have led to that, which explained his actions.

Dardanos, content that I understood, continued. "The king decided to raid the rich gold mines in the mountains east of Apulum. On our journey, king Tarbus reconciled with my lord Thiaper. He called him into his tent and apologized. I heard it with my own ears, lord."

It did not sound like the Tarbus I knew, but I had no reason to doubt the words of Dardanos.

"We travelled fast, lord. Lord Tarbus and his oathsworn scouted the way. Before the Romans could muster their warriors, we slipped past their fort at Apulum. The mines were well-defended but we prevailed, even though we lost many brave warriors."

"Our saddlebags were heavy with looted gold. It seemed that the gods favoured us, lord. That is until we tried to return home. The Romans had dug a ditch across the pass. The barrier had a rampart and stakes, much the same as at Rucar. Same artillery as well."

This did not come as a surprise as it was what I expected.

"We were running out of food. One out of three warriors who came to this land has gone to Tengri, lord. There were not enough warriors to storm the wall and defeat the Romans."

"Then the king went to speak with the great Roman general. Lord Decius is his name. King Tarbus returned safely. The Roman general and the king came to an agreement. If a Carpiani were to defeat the Roman champion, he would let us go with half the gold. If not, we would lay down our weapons and become slaves. Lord Tarbus paid the Roman lord even before the champions fought."

"The king chose lord Thiaper as his champion. It was a good choice, and a great honour for my lord."

"Did you witness the fight, Dardanos?"

"I saw all of it. Lord Thiaper fought like a god, but the Roman..." he struggled to find the right words. "The Roman fought in a way I have never seen before. He wore no armour, but he moved like lightning, cutting up my lord piece by piece. But the Roman slipped somehow, before my lord was done for, and he died on the blade of a Carpiani sword."

"The Romans were distracted while the champions fought. Lord Tarbus had us attack the wall and we easily breached it. Suppose he did not trust the Romans to keep their end of the bargain."

I was baffled by the deal Decius had agreed to. Why would he allow Tarbus to leave with half the gold? Why not just destroy the Carpiani?

I abandoned that line of thought and enquired after the health of my friend. "And your lord? Has he made a full recovery?"

"He is still very ill, lord. We are not allowed to see him. The shaman of the king is treating his wounds. Some of the nobles loyal to Lord Thiaper blame the king for his injuries, but while my lord is alive, they have hope, and will remain with the army."

The story seemed odd in more than one way, but I realised that I would arouse suspicion and create further problems by asking too many questions.

I had one last question for him. "Are you being pursued by the Romans?"

"They are but two days' march behind us, lord. The Carpiani horde will reach where we are now before the sun sets this evening."

"Dardanos of the Carpiani, go now and inform your king that you have found the army of the Goths and the Roxolani", I said, dismissing him. I turned my horse and trotted back to join the Huns.

The arrival of the Carpiani was important news that had to reach the ears of the kings. We rode back to the camp at a gallop, only stopping to change and water the horses. It was late afternoon when we eventually returned, our tired bodies covered with dust.

The barbarian army had not been idle, as their camp was ten miles closer to the Danube. Gordas, Hostilius and I found Bradakos outside his tent, still on his horse. Despite being the king, he had led the Roxolani scouting party that reconnoitred towards the east.

We were ushered into the king's tent. At his command, slaves served us watered down white wine in enormous silver mugs. We all drank thirstily, wetting our parched throats.

We were hardly seated on the soft furs when Elmanos and Marcus entered, equally dusty from their mission south. They accepted the watered wine and greedily gulped it down, both wiping their beards with the back of their hands as they sat down. I managed to hide my amusement at the similarities between the cultured Roman equestrian and the barbarian noble.

The king nodded and looked straight at Elmanos. "Lord, we have located the emperor and two legions to the south. They are but two days' march behind us."

It was my turn to report. "We have located the Carpiani. Tonight they will camp thirty miles west of here. A Roman army follows two days behind. There is more, but it is a long story."

Bradakos held up his hand. "I would hear it all, Eochar, but first, we too have found a Roman army. Two legions, two days' march from here."

We knew that the Romans were closing the jaws of the trap.

"Bradakos, I was told an unsettling tale today. Our friend Thiaper is seriously wounded. Even worse, I believe that Tarbus is hatching a plan that is less than savoury."

At the mention of the name of the king of the Carpiani, a scowl appeared on my mentor's face, his mood suddenly dark.

"Tell us", said the king.

So I did.

Hostilius spoke first. "Let me try to get this right. Our friend Thiaper defies Tarbus in front of the warriors. Tarbus, the wise, forgives him. Then the Carpiani king gets himself trapped and Decius, the kind Roman senator, lets him off the hook. Unlucky for Thiaper, he is seriously wounded, but the kind king's shaman is looking after him all good and proper."

Hostilius downed the content of his second mug of wine. "Not bloody likely."

"Let me tell you what I think really happened."

"Thiaper is a noble of the Carpiani. An honest man, a formidable fighter, and most importantly, he's got the support of the lesser nobles as well as the warriors. Our man starts to stand up to Tarbus, who is shit scared that Thiaper might challenge him to single combat. He's too cautious to order Thiaper's death, as there is a chance his own men may turn against him and kill him in the process."

257

Hostilius grinned, getting into the swing of the story. "Tarbus is a sly bastard, so he acts like he's forgiven Thiaper. It also raises his esteem in the eyes of the warriors. Then he takes his oathsworn and meets with the snake Decius while they were supposed to be scouting the lay of the land."

"Decius allows Tarbus to 'slip' through to the mines, where he fills his saddlebags with gold. As payment, Decius gets to keep half the gold, but he won't tell the emperor about his windfall. He makes it look like the Carpiani breached the wall while the champions were fighting and that they escaped with all the looted gold."

"In addition, the Roman champion was supposed to kill Thiaper, solving another problem for Tarbus, but he gets lucky and survives. He's keeping our friend alive to bind the errant nobles to the army. Once they cross the river, he'll kill Thiaper."

Hostilius smiled triumphantly. "Tell me I'm wrong."

We all stared at him, dumbfounded.

It turned out he was right, or almost right, yet we did not realise how deep the treachery lay.

Chapter 33 – Enaree

Apart from the strange behaviour of the Carpiani king and Hostilius's elaborate theory there was another, more pressing, problem to address.

"We need to slow down the advance of the Roman armies or they will fall on our rear while the wagons cross the river. Give me your thoughts so I can discuss them with the Gothic kings." Bradakos sat back, waiting for us to respond.

"Keep it simple", Hostilius suggested. "We divide the Scythian horse warriors into two warbands of three-and-a-half thousand each. Each warband will attack a Roman force. The Romans will end up forming the testudo so we won't kill many, but we will buy enough time for the wagons to cross the ford. Ostrogotha and Kniva can send a message to their puppet Tarbus to harry the Roman force pursuing the Carpiani."

He drank from his cup. "Simple, eh?"

In my own mind I was working on an elaborate plan to slow down the advancing Roman armies, but there was something else that had to be done, so I said: "I like your plan, Primus Pilus, but I would like to suggest that we make two small changes."

Before he could reply, I added: "Firstly, I request that the king excuse us from this mission." A frown creased Hostilius's face and I continued. "That includes you, Primus Pilus."

"Secondly, I would like to borrow Gordas and his men."

* * *

The Carpiani had arrived in Roman lands with five thousand warriors. No more than three-and-a-half thousand remained. Tarbus cared little for the lives of his men.

I lay on my stomach at the edge of the treeline of a copse overlooking the Carpiani camp. Gordas and Hostilius lay next to me. Marcus, Vibius and Cai were farther back, keeping an eye on the horses.

We watched as Tarbus left the camp at the head of a warband I estimated to number three thousand.

Ostrogotha sent Tarbus a message, requesting him to harass and slow down the Roman army approaching from the west along the Danube. As the Carpiani owed fealty to the Goths, he was expected to comply.

I earlier discussed my plan with Ostrogotha in private, seeking permission from the Gothic king. "I have met the shaman of the Carpiani king. He is a snake, Eochar. For the sake of honour, I hope you succeed." Then he added with a grin: "There is one condition, though. I demand to be told the tale on your return."

In any event, we patiently waited until a quarter of a watch had passed. Then we stealthily retrieved the horses and joined the rest of the Hun warband which was concealed in a nearby valley.

With the king gone, my companions and I confidently rode at the head of five hundred Urugundi, heading for the camp of the Carpiani.

Not long after, we were intercepted by a patrol. Their leader, a lesser noble and oathsworn of Tarbus, called Ziaka, eyed us suspiciously.

I assumed he knew our faces. "Welcome to the camp of the Carpiani, my lords", he said smoothly.

I nodded. "We have come to speak with king Tarbus, Ziaka. I gestured towards Cai, who wore his face of stone. A renowned healer from the lands of Serica accompany us. He has volunteered his services to the king."

A confused expression settled on the face of the Carpiani warrior, exactly as I had planned.

"Lead the way, Ziaka", I said, and kicked my horse past him, followed closely by the five hundred Huns.

Ziaka fell in beside me. "Lord, the king is not in camp", he said, an edge of panic discernible in his voice.

"Do not concern yourself, Ziaka, I will visit with my friend, Lord Thiaper", I said.

Ziaka was aware of my reputation. He tried to persuade me to abandon the visit to my friend, without offending me, of course. I ignored his words.

He briefly glanced at Gordas and Hostilius, hoping to find support. On witnessing the dour expressions carried by the great Roman and Hun lords, he rode at my side in silence, having accepted the inevitable.

"Tell me about the healer who is tending to the needs of Lord Thiaper", I said.

"Decaeneus is a powerful shaman, an enaree, lord. His name means, 'the one who knows'".

Allow me to digress. Many generations ago, it is said, Scythians pillaged the temple of the goddess Agrimpasa, the one the Greeks call Aphrodite. The goddess bestowed on these transgressors the power of divination, but commanded that they would for all eternity be women, trapped inside the bodies of men. These men were known as enarees.

"Good, then he will be expecting us", I said, adding to Ziaka's confusion.

As was the custom, I left the Hun warband outside the Carpiani camp.

I dismounted and strode confidently into the tented camp. Hostilius, Marcus and Cai followed. Ziaka all but ran to catch up with us.

The warriors who remained were tasked with striking camp and escorting the wagons. They were focused on the task, paying us no heed.

Our guide slowed down as we neared the centre of the camp. He stopped, too fearful to approach, and pointed to a large tent ten paces away. "It is the tent of the enaree, lord." He swallowed. "Decaeneus will not look kindly upon this unannounced intrusion."

"Do not be concerned, Ziaka. Wait here", I ordered.

Hostilius and I entered the tent, while Marcus and Cai remained outside, guarding the door.

I opened the flap and thick white smoke escaped from within. It was the familiar fumes associated with the burning of hemp seeds, used by kings and shamans. As my eyes adjusted to the low light, I noticed the enaree sitting crossed-legged on an old bear fur in the centre of the tent. His eyes were closed while

263

he swayed to and fro, chanting indiscernible words. The feathers of some bird were knotted into his near-black hair, eerily contrasting his white-painted face. My attention was drawn to his hands, which he held in front of his body. Strands of tree bark were braided around his fingers, assisting him in his dreamwork.

I had grown up with the Scythians and suddenly found that I was reluctant to interrupt the enaree, who was obviously deep in shamanic trance.

Hostilius had no such qualms. "Hey, you", he shouted.

The shaman stood, his eyes still closed, and untangled the bark from between his fingers. I heard a low moan emanate from the far side of the tent and saw the prone body of my friend.

Thiaper's hands were bound, as were his feet. Rage welled up from deep inside my stomach. The enaree opened his eyes. "Who dares disturb the servant of Agrimpasa?" he screeched in a high-pitched voice, so typical of his sect. "You are cursed for all eternity", he continued, and came at me with a dagger.

My main concern was to not kill him instantly, as that would complicate the situation. I blocked the blow of the small poisoned blade with my left arm. The metal strips of my vambrace numbed his arm, the blade clattering onto the smoke-stones. My right hand remained open as it struck his neck at the base of the skull. The little shaman collapsed at my feet.

I called out to Cai, who entered the tent.

While Cai was tending to Thiaper we sat the shaman upright. Hostilius poured liquid, which we erroneously assumed to be water, over his head and his eyes flickered open.

I sat down in front of the man and Hostilius joined me. "Decaeneus, do you know that the Carpiani is bound to the Goths?" He nodded, a smirk on his face.

Hostilius played with the little dagger, which made the brutish Roman appear even more menacing. The shaman's eyes flicked to the blade every few heartbeats.

"The king of the Goths owes me a favour, Decaeneus, but you knew that, didn't you?"

He still looked at me defiantly. "Ostrogotha the Patient will ask his vassal, King Tarbus, to send you to the Greuthungi. To assist with divinations, of course." The little man lost his smirk.

"There, Decaeneus, you will be my guest."

Cai said from the back of the tent, speaking in Scythian: "Thiaper not good. Maybe too late to save."

I gripped the dirty skins of the enaree and drew him towards me, nearly onto the blade Hostilius was still playing with. "I have seen the Urugundi keep a man alive for ten days after removing his lower jaw. They have to use fire every day, else the victim bleeds out."

Decaeneus was coming around to our cause, I believed.

"You will tell king Tarbus that king Ostrogotha has sent for Thiaper. Tell him that you have given Thiaper poison and that he will surely die. Weave a convincing tale and you might just stay alive. Else, the king of the Goths will send for you."

The shaman nodded, realising that he had no choice.

"Divine your own future, enaree", I added. "Then you will see in the bark that Eochar the Merciless does not make empty threats."

Cai wrapped Thiaper in a cloak. Hostilius was as strong as an ox, throwing the bulky Carpiani over his shoulder as if he were a child.

We ducked out of the tent, coming face to face with Ziaka. "The enaree has given your lord over into the care of the man from Serica. It has been foretold by the gods."

He nodded in wide-eyed reverence, and briskly led us from the camp.

* * *

I have often wondered whether our actions on that day contributed to what would come to pass. There is no way to know. My only consolation is that all, in the end, was the will of Arash.

Chapter 34 – Crossing (October 245 AD)

We harassed the Roman legions for two more days until all the Gothic wagons had crossed the ford in the river. Most of the Roxolani warriors had only a handful of arrows left in their quivers when they eventually ascended the northern bank of the Danube.

The nearest Roman army was a day's march behind, but still there was no sign of the Carpiani.

"Their tardiness will cost them their lives", Bradakos said. He stared across to the southern bank, shielding his eyes with his hand.

"They will be here within a third of a watch", I said. "The scouts have confirmed it."

Bradakos was not done. "They are tardy because of their greed. They have loaded all their wagons with loot. When a wheel comes off or an axle breaks, they repair it and the whole army is held up. The Goths have many spare wagons. They have mastered their greed. It is as it should be."

"How is Thiaper?" he asked.

"His wounds are red and angry and he has the burning sickness", I replied. "Cai has little hope."

"Has he told his tale?" the king asked.

"Thiaper is halfway between the world of man and the realm of the gods, my friend. His words make no sense. He is travelling in a comfortable wagon with Kniva's entourage. Cai is with him all the time. More we cannot do."

Bradakos pointed to activity on the southern bank of the river. "It seems our friend Tarbus has arrived."

A lone horsemen detached from the advance group of Carpiani and started across the river. "Seems like Tarbus has a message for us", I said.

Before long the scout made his way to where we were waiting. The king's guards barred his way, but Bradakos waved them away.

The scout dismounted and approached on foot. He went down on both knees and bowed low.

"Lord, king Tarbus sends his best wishes. The king thanks great king Bradakos and his brave warriors for keeping the Romans at bay. He says that the Romans are still far away and that he does not require any further assistance, lord. The Carpiani will start the crossing soon."

Bradakos nodded. "Go now. Tell your king that the Goths and the Roxolani will continue their journey. He should send us a message if he is in need of our warriors."

269

The king turned his horse, the guards falling in behind him.

Gordas and the Urugundi scouted far and wide. Until we crossed the limes and the adjoining Alutus River, we were still on Roman soil.

We travelled east through countryside that had been raided by the Roxolani months before. The horse warriors had left their mark on the land. We passed half-burnt farmhouses and followed the Roman roads through once prosperous little towns and settlements, now deserted.

Once or twice we encountered brave souls who had returned to their dwellings. Unsurprisingly they fled at our approach. Bradakos issued an order for these people to be left to their own devices. Not all the warriors agreed, but they knew that ignoring the king's commands would be at their peril.

The Limes Transalutanus was deserted, as we expected it to be. It took us half a day to create a breach in the fortifications before we could start to cross the river.

Again, there was no sign of the Carpiani. We only received word when our outriders made contact with their advance scouts. Our scouts were told that all was well and that the Romans were still pursuing the Carpiani, but falling farther behind.

The constant care Thiaper received from Cai was finally paying off. He was healing, but his left leg still carried an angry wound. Although he was still delirious, his condition was much improved.

On the fifth evening after we had entered the tribal lands of the Roxolani, we were summoned to a gathering in the tent of king Ostrogotha the Patient.

It would be a feast meant for generals and kings. Hostilius, Marcus and I were invited. Cai nursed Thiaper, and Vibius was more than content to join the Roxolani. I was sure that he had his eye on a lithe female warrior, which he vehemently denied.

"We are just friends, Eochar. Why can't a man and a woman be friends?"

It was all nonsense of course, as I noticed the way he looked at her.

Just after sunset we arrived at the tent of the king of the Greuthungi Goths. Even though we were early, we were ushered into the presence of the king.

Ostrogotha sat on a low stool on the far side of the tent. It was late autumn and the weather was chilly. He wore a long-sleeved tunic of undyed wool. His sword and dagger were attached to a magnificent red leather belt edged with fine silver wire. Around his broad shoulders hung a soft fur cloak made of the pelts of wolves.

Over the years, I have met many kings and rulers. It is not an easy task to create the appearance of regality without sacrificing the warrior aura. Ostrogotha succeeded in this regard. He truly was a kingly warrior.

"You and your companions are welcome to enjoy my hospitality this night, Prince Eochar", he said, while slaves showed us where to sit.

We sat down on the soft furs. Slaves brought wooden platters heaped with freshly roasted beef and wildfowl. I was offered a horn of ale, but I declined, gesturing to the pitcher undoubtedly filled with looted wine.

Kniva and Bradakos arrived moments later.

The Roxolani king was accompanied by Gordas and Elmanos. Strangely Guntharic, the Greuthungi general, accompanied my brother-in-law.

The king stood and raised his ale-horn. "Tonight, we feast. The gods have blessed our campaign."

He drank deeply from the horn, wiping the foam from his blonde beard with the back of his hand. "Before we get drunk, friends", he said, "I have another announcement to make."

"Rise Kniva, son of Ostrogotha", he said.

Kniva stood proudly.

"Kniva, iudex of the mighty Thervingi, will from this day on be as my son", Ostrogotha announced.

All present cheered.

"From this day on, the enemy of the Thervingi will be the enemy of the Greuthungi. Your allies will be my allies. This I swear before all, as Teiwaz is my witness."

My brother-in-law grinned proudly as his father-in-law continued to heap praise upon him.

That night a power was created that would shake the very foundations of Rome. In time, my brother-in-law's name would echo through the ages. Sadly greatness always comes at a cost.

When Ostrogotha was done speaking, he gestured in the direction of the entrance. The royal bard walked in and bowed low to all present.

The man was well-groomed, and intelligence shone from his eyes. He weaved a tale of Goths and Scythians fighting side by side. He sang about warriors who, through their bravery and cunning, defeated the evil that is Rome. Our deeds were greatly exaggerated. I was depicted as the favourite of the god of war and fire, the messenger of Arash. Before long, the tunes would be sung by the common folk, and our reputation would spread across the land.

It was a fitting conclusion to a successful campaign. The wine flowed freely late into the evening as we shared stories, sang songs and forged relationships.

Come morning, the armies of the Goths and Roxolani readied to each go their own way. The Roxolani would travel due north to the winter camp of their king. The Thervingi and the Greuthungi would travel together until they reached Kniva's lands. From there Ostrogotha would still have a few days in the saddle before he reached his home.

Gordas sought me out. "Eochar, your people need to see you. The common folk have all heard of your deeds, but they desire to lay their eyes upon the messenger of Arash, beloved of the god of war and fire. Bradakos would greatly appreciate it if you would visit, even if only for a day or two."

I narrowed my eyes. "Gordas, you sound like Bradakos. Did he put you up to it?"

He waved away my remark. "Spend two days with us, my friend, then we will escort you to the lands of the Goths. You might even be there before they arrive. We will ride like the wind." He grinned like a boy at the prospect.

I was desperate to see my family, but I knew Gordas was right. I could visit with the Roxolani and still be home before the encumbered army of the Goths.

"I will speak with my friends first, Gordas", I said.

I found Hostilius just outside the camp of the IV Italica. "King Ostrogotha has given the men sanctuary. They will remain in the lands of the Greuthungi for now."

He walked closer to me until his face was but half an arm's length away from mine. Hostilius looked me in the eye, and I must confess that I felt intimidated. But his reason was all but that. "Lucius, these men will not forget what you have done for them. I... I will not forget either. When Rome spurned their loyalty, you returned their honour. They are whole again."

I wanted to ask him about a visit to the Roxolani, but I discarded the thought. I placed my hand on his armoured shoulder. "Hostilius, you are like a brother to me."

Chapter 35 – Nomad camp

Cai did not blink an eye when I suggested a brief visit to the Roxolani camp. His lack of surprise immediately made me suspicious.

"Did you foresee this?" I asked.

"No. Gordas say he go convince you. Say it easy. See he right."

Cai pointed towards the wagons of the Goths. "I stay with Thiaper in wagon. He talk soon."

It turned out that Marcus, Vibius and Hostilius were already informed. All arranged by Gordas. I felt mildly cheated and went to confront Gordas who was nowhere to be found, of course.

I ended up joining Bradakos's entourage, planning to complain about my Hun friend.

"Eochar, my heart feels good that you have made time for your mother's people", Bradakos said. "They see your visits as good omens. It means a lot to the Roxolani."

"Thank you for inviting me, my friend", I heard myself say, Gordas suddenly forgotten.

The Roxolani had sent their loot home before they crossed the Danube, nearly four moons earlier. Therefore there was no reason to tarry, allowing us to give free rein to the horses.

After two days of hard riding, we entered the Scythian winter camp. The loot had long since arrived, with some already distributed to the families of the warriors, in accordance with the instructions of the king.

The nomads gathered outside their tents and wagons. They cheered the arrival of the king, their sons, daughters, husbands and wives.

The following evening, Bradakos laid on a great feast for the people. Numerous sheep were spitted over open fires, and the warriors were welcomed back as all-conquering heroes.

I spent time walking amongst the warriors, reliving the battles fought while on campaign, and toasting their deeds of bravery.

It was truly a fine evening.

I went to bed content with my decision to visit with my mother's people, and looking forward to be reunited with my wife and daughter. I made up my mind to tell Bradakos that we would depart the next day.

Hostilius woke me. "Domitius, better come quickly."

It was bitterly cold. I pulled on my deerskin boots and donned my sheepskin overcoat.

277

We were ushered into the tent of the king and found Bradakos in conversation with a warrior. The man, whose back was turned to us, was on his knees in front of the king.

From his clothing he was easily identifiable as a Carpiani. The man turned around and we came face to face with Dardanos.

He inclined his head. "Greetings, lord", he said.

I nodded, realising that it was not a courtesy visit. My first thought was that the incident with Thiaper and the enaree had come home to roost. Of course I was wrong.

"Tell him", the king said, and motioned with his hand for Dardanos to continue. "And for the sake of the gods, get up, man."

Dardanos awkwardly came to his feet. "Lord Eochar", he said, "the Carpiani horde has been trapped by the Romans. King Tarbus begs for the assistance of the Roxolani."

"Tell us all", I said.

"It was four days ago, lord. Our army crossed the border fortifications of Dacia. The king received reports that the legions did not cross into the tribal lands. We all heard that the Romans had ceased their pursuit. We were happy that the danger had passed." A servant handed him a cup of watered wine and he gratefully accepted, drinking thirstily.

He wiped his beard with his hand. "But the Romans were clever, lord. They sent an army of horsemen to ambush us. Not Romans sir, but African and Germani horsemen, lord. We fought back and were able to find refuge within a hillfort used by the old people of this land. Many Carpiani have gone to the sky-father, lord, but there are at least two thousand men left. We have blocked the access by felling trees. The enemy horsemen cannot attack us, but we will run out of food soon. There are only three thousand of the enemy. If you send three thousand warriors, lord, we will easily crush them."

As an afterthought he added. "We are all saddened by the news of the death of lord Thiaper, lord. Now this has happened." He hung his head. "The gods have surely deserted us."

"Wait outside, Dardanos. I will discuss this with Lord Eochar", Bradakos said.

Dardanos bowed low and was escorted outside by a guard.

Hostilius was first to speak. "He wasn't lying. I can smell lies."

I wanted to speak but the Primus Pilus held up his hand.

"Something feels out of place. Why would Tarbus ask for your help, Bradakos? He despises you. And the whole story with Thiaper? Remember Tarbus's meeting with Decius. It's all connected somehow, I tell you. If you want my advice, just look the other way and leave that conniving snake at the mercy of the bloody Romans."

"You are right about Tarbus, Centurion. He is a snake and I am not concerned about him. What does concern me, however, is the fate of two thousand Carpiani warriors. They will run out of food. Eventually they will have to surrender. The Romans will enslave them all. That I cannot allow."

He thought for a moment and continued. "There is no time to recall the Goths. The Roxolani will have to aid the Carpiani."

Unbeknown to us, Kniva and the Thervingi horde were already on their way.

"I will summon the warriors. We ride tomorrow", he said.

"Allow me to gather the Huns", I added.

Bradakos placed his hand on my shoulder. "You have done enough, Eochar. More than enough. Go to your wife and your family. The Roxolani will chase the Roman auxiliaries away and win the gratitude of the Carpiani. It might even solve the issue we have with Tarbus. This is not your fight, nor will I involve Gordas."

There was no arguing with the king. Later that same day, Hostilius, Marcus and I watched as Bradakos rode from camp, accompanied by three thousand of his best horse archers. Soon after we departed for the lands of the Goths, excited to return home. Gordas and fifty of his men volunteered to escort us while still in Roxolani territory.

We only had a watch of daylight left and did not travel far before the light started to fade. There was no need to risk injury to the horses and we set up camp for the night. We lit fires inside the tents, as was the norm during winter. A howling wind announced the onset of a bout of even colder weather and we huddled inside the tents, drank mead and added fresh meat and roots to boiling water. Before long we were wolfing down the delicious broth.

Marcus poured another helping of broth into his bowl and pulled his wolf pelt cloak tighter around his shoulders.

Our Hun horses were tethered downwind from the tent to afford them some shelter. These creatures were hardy, able to withstand the harsh conditions on the Sea of Grass.

Then, from nowhere, horses started neighing in panic, followed by a commotion outside. I grabbed my strung bow and three arrows. Just then Gordas poked his head into the tent.

"No need to come outside Eochar. Good news is, Tengri has given us twelve wolf pelts." I heard a yelp coming from the darkness. "Thirteen wolf pelts", he corrected himself.

With the wolves taken care of, we settled down again.

Hostilius summarised it well. "We have had a successful campaign. Our brothers in the IV Italica have a temporary home. Our saddlebags are filled with gold."

I nodded to show my agreement with Hostilius's words.

"Then tell me, why do I feel uneasy?" he said.

I shrugged. "It happens at the end of a campaign", I said, trying to explain away my own anxiety.

Sleep did not come easily and I prayed to Arash to give me a vision of the future.

That night, the god of war and fire chose to keep me in the dark.

Chapter 36 – Lone rider

The storm cleared overnight, leaving bright blue skies.

The first real cold of winter put a spring in the step of my Hun friend. "Tengri favours us with good weather", he said, and strapped a couple of solidly frozen wolfskins onto his packhorse.

"I will have a cloak made for you, Eochar. It will be ready when you return."

"I may not come this way for many moons, my friend", I said.

Before long we were on our way, cantering north and east at an easy pace. It was the second watch of the morning. We crested a low hill, allowing us a panoramic view of the unending grassland beyond.

Gordas reined in his horse, the rest of his men following suit.

He walked his horse towards me, pointing his finger in the direction of the wide expanse of grass. "A man is approaching. He is riding like the wind of the plains."

I shielded my eyes from the glare of the sun. In the distance I noticed a speck, a small dust cloud in its wake.

It was not the nature of the Huns to be patient. "Let us ride and see why this stranger is in such a hurry", he said, and kicked his horse into a gallop.

We cantered down the gentle slope in the direction of the lone rider who turned his horse towards us when he noticed our approach.

My heart jumped in my throat when I recognized the loose-flowing robes of the horseman fluttering as he galloped into view.

Cai was drenched in sweat, his face a mask of stone. "Thiaper talk. It not good", he said

My friend from Serica told his story.

Thiaper's wounds had healed. Shortly after the burning sickness left him, he returned to the world of man and told his tale to Cai.

* * *

Thiaper fought the champion of Decius. He was losing badly. The expert Roman swordsman cut him up piece by piece.

Tarbus and Decius watched, the Carpiani king as unconcerned as the gloating Roman.

When it seemed that Thiaper's fate was sealed, Tarbus leaned in to where my friend was bleeding his lifeblood away into the dust.

With a smirk Tarbus informed him of his plans, sure that Thiaper would take it with him into the afterlife. "This is the price the gods demand for your treachery, Thiaper. You will die today. You, who favour the Roxolani above your own people. The Carpiani has gained the favour of Rome. Your friends Bradakos and Eochar will die at the hands of Philip the Arab. I have been paid well to make the arrangements."

Shortly after, the Roman stumbled and Fortuna granted Thiaper the victory.

* * *

Dardanos earlier told us what had transpired after the fight

Hostilius put it to words. "Bloody bastard! Now it all fits. Philip the Arab plans to fall onto an unsuspecting Bradakos. He wins a great victory, then rushes back to Rome, all covered in glory. Having beaten the Scythians, his critics will be silenced, and his popularity will soar. He will demand a triumph and claim some or other elaborate official title like 'Carpicus Maximus' or something of the sort."

I turned cold on the inside as I recalled the words of the old woman in the woods. The words of warning which I had discarded as the ramblings of a peasant. *"Beware the one who begs assistance, trust not the one who makes the peace."*

I ignored the message from the gods and now my friend and mentor was in mortal danger while I was many miles away.

Cai drank from his waterskin. "Kniva on his way. Ten thousand men on horses. Ostrogotha also come with elite warriors. Maybe two thousand more. But they slow. Not ride like Huns."

Gordas listened intently. "We ride to warn the king?"

I nodded.

"It will be quicker if it is only you and me", he said.

"We will each take three spare horses. The best we have. We will ride so fast that the steppe wind, the buran, will not catch us."

I turned to my friends. "Find Kniva, then ride to the Roxolani camp. The Huns will guide you. Follow the trail of the Roxolani army and pray to the gods we find them in time."

Gordas shouted instructions to his men, who brought six horses, three for each of us. I tied the rope holding the horses to the horn on my saddle, and kicked Simsek to a gallop. Gordas was alongside, grinning. "Today we will see if you can hold your own against a Hun." He leaned forward, his head close to his horse's mane. Gordas whispered, and the horse, sensing the urgency, accelerated. I also leaned forward, as I had learned all those years ago, and told Simsek that we ride to save the king. We all but flew.

The sun was setting when we arrived at the Roxolani tented village. We rode directly to where the Huns made their camp.

Gordas shouted commands to his warriors and they rushed to see to our needs.

"We take fresh horses", he said, "and five hundred of the men. But first we rest." I started to complain, and he held up his hand. "If you fall off the horse, you will be of no help to Bradakos. I will send two of my best warriors ahead on the fastest horses we have."

While the Huns prepared to go to war, Gordas and I lay down on the comfortable furs in his tent. We did not bother to remove our armour, yet we fell asleep almost immediately.

Simsek thundered down a long, sloping hill, the sound of his hooves like a smith pounding the impurities from a virgin piece of iron. Underneath my legs I felt his flanks moving like bellows, forcing air into his lungs. I stroked his muscular neck, whispering words of encouragement. Then I glanced ahead.

Arrayed in the distance were thousands of horsemen deployed in a line that stretched into eternity. Their red cloaks fluttered in the breeze and I knew they were Romans. I glanced to the left, then to the right, but of the army I had expected to see, there was no sign. My eyes moved to the right. Again, there was no one. Then the pounding of the hooves increased in intensity and I glanced over my shoulder. I saw an enormous black stallion powering from behind.

The eyes of the god shone bright and blue, his silver bow strung, an arrow nocked. He met my gaze. He wore a full face conical helmet of silver with a plume of black horsehair. I could not see his face, but his eyes were smiling, relishing the prospect of imminent battle.

I turned my eyes to the front once more, but the enemy had vanished.

In the distance I saw a city surrounded by immense walls. The likes of which I had never laid eyes on.

I woke with a start.

Gordas was shaking my leg in an effort to wake me.

"Time to go, the warriors are ready", he said.

I stood and walked from the tent without saying a word. Deep down I was reeling, still unbalanced by the vision of the god of war and fire.

It was not yet light, but the promise of a bright day could be seen on the eastern horizon.

I jumped onto the magnificent horse which Gordas had arranged for me and took the rope with the two spare horses attached.

My Urugundi friend and I set a gruelling pace, even measured by the standard of the Huns. Our horses devoured the miles and we stopped only to rest and water them, changing mounts at the gallop.

It would take the Roxolani three days to reach the Carpiani. We were a day behind. I prayed to Fortuna to delay the passage of the Scythians. Only with the intervention of the gods would we be able to reach them in time.

We rode late into the evening, until horses collapsed from fatigue. We camped without erecting tents or lighting fires, sleeping next to our mounts, wrapped in furs.

Come morning, we departed long before the sun showed itself. We rode like men possessed.

By midday on the second day after leaving camp, Gordas appeared next to me.

"Eochar, we are but a watch away from where we expect the Carpiani to be."

I nodded, urging on my horse.

A third of a watch passed when we met up with the two Hun scouts, riding towards us. We did not rein in, but allowed them to give their report while we thundered on.

"There is a great battle up ahead, lord. The Roxolani warriors are surrounded by thousands of Roman riders. They are outnumbered three to one. Tarbus's men have not joined the fight yet, lord. They are watching from the earthen rampart. We do not understand, lord."

"Beware the one who makes the peace", I muttered to myself, drawing a questioning glance from Gordas.

"Tarbus, the snake, has accepted a payment of peace", I said.

Gordas shook his head. "Surely that cannot be, he has taken the oath of blood?"

Soon we could hear the unmistakeable sounds of battle emanating from the valley just beyond the next gentle hill.

The time for stealth had passed. We crested the hill and took in the scene. The Scythians were surrounded, desperately trying to break free from the ever-tightening noose of Roman horsemen. On the hill overlooking the valley, I saw the Carpiani watch from the age-old earthen walls.

Without hesitation we powered on, Gordas reading my mind. "We will form a wedge and strike deep into their formation. Just mayhap we can save our friends."

With a signal of Gordas's hand, the five hundred Huns arranged themselves into an arrow formation, with Gordas and myself at the tip. I reached for my strung bow, taking three arrows in my draw hand. The Romans were fully embroiled in the fight. It took all their skill and attention to hem the Scythians in for the slaughter. They did not notice our approach until it was too late.

At a hundred paces from the rear of the Roman line, I released my arrows in rapid succession with a near-flat trajectory. All the Huns along the outer edge of the formation did the same, concentrating their arrows along a frontage of thirty paces, the width of the formation. The warriors at the centre of the wedge released overhead, the projectiles striking the Romans from above.

I emptied a full quiver, the Roman formation breaking as the armour-piercing arrows penetrated the chain mail of the auxiliaries. The last of my arrows I released at point blank range. Next would be close quarter work. I gripped my Sasanian mace in my right hand, my left hand finding the shaft of my battle-axe.

A burly warrior turned his horse to face me and the spike of my axe struck the side of his helmet mid-turn. Stunned, he slipped off his horse and disappeared under the hooves. More of the enemy turned to come to grips with the new threat. A young auxiliary pulled back his spear to strike, but a lasso snatched him from his horse, his screams fading away as we advanced. A broad-headed spear snaked from behind a shield. I deflected it with my heavy mace, the spearpoint scraping along the scales of my armour. I drew back my mace and repeatedly hammered at the spearman who hid behind his splintered shield, trying to absorb the blows. A piece of his helmet appeared, and with the next blow a flange ripped it open, taking him out of the fight. Another spear came at me but Gordas's axe severed the iron head. The haft struck my armour harmlessly while Gordas sent him on his way.

A black-bearded giant in leather armour came at me with a longsword. He swung overhead, a mighty blow. I had no shield, so I dropped my axe and grabbed the other end of my iron-shafted mace. His powerful blow was blocked by the shaft, but it numbed my hands. Grinning he drew back again, and I parried in the same way. The mace fell from my hands. He drew back to finish me off but tumbled forward, a Roxolani spear imbedded between his shoulderblades.

We turned our horses and fought our way to freedom, the surviving Roxolani following in our wake.

The auxiliaries turned in pursuit, but soon realised their folly as they fell to the arrows of the nomads. The buccina signalled, and the Romans wisely abandoned the chase.

I reined in on an open stretch of ground, at least five miles away from the enemy. Gordas's signifier signalled the halt. Soon the Huns and Roxolani were milling about on their horses.

Half of the Roxolani who rode from camp three days before had perished in the ambush. I feverishly tried to locate Bradakos, but ended up face to face with Elmanos.

His expression was one that told of despair.

"Where is the king, Elmanos?" I asked, fearing the answer.

He hung his head. "The king fell, Lord Eochar. I do not believe that he is dead, though. I saw him being dragged away, to the rear."

"I tried to save him, lord, but there were just too many." Then I noticed blood dripping down his leg onto the grass.

"Lie down, Elmanos, I will see to your wound", I commanded.

"It is not that bad", he began, but I was angry and frustrated. "Do as I say, Elmanos, son of Masas", I growled.

He knew better than to gainsay me and allowed me to examine the gash in his upper thigh. I poured vinegar and honey on the wound and bound it with linen. "Do not blame yourself, Elmanos", I said.

"I had been forewarned by the gods, but I ignored them because of my hubris", I added, and felt a stab of guilt at hearing the truth from my own tongue.

Gordas appeared from the mill of men. "We have lost one in five", he said. "But they have left this world with honour. They saved the lives of many and will be accepted into the presence of the war god."

I nodded in agreement with his words. "The king has been taken, Gordas."

"My friend, to die in battle while facing the enemy is a great honour", the Hun replied. "To fight and die bravely when the odds are insurmountable is truly a gift from the gods." He cast his eyes downward. "A brave warrior such as Bradakos of the Roxolani deserves better than to die a slave."

For once, I was the voice of reason. "Let us camp for the night and look after the wounded. Tomorrow we will devise a plan."

I assisted in treating the wounds of the warriors. I am no healer, but Cai had taught me the basics over the years. Exhausted and dispirited I lay down on the furs, too tired to remove my armour. I blamed myself for discarding the advice of the old crone.

What did the vision mean that I had received from Arash the night before?

Chapter 37 – Parley

I woke feeling disheartened.

Gordas and Elmanos came to see me. They were both in a bad way.

"Only two hundred of my men are fit to ride today. Maybe twenty more if I count the wounded who are still able to draw a bow", Gordas said.

"Half of my men who survived cannot fight, although they are willing", Elmanos added. "A thousand warriors are able to fight, although most carry injuries."

We tried, but could not come up with a viable plan.

"What of the Goths?" I asked.

"I sent out scouts this morning, but they are yet to return. The Goth army is huge, it will move slowly. They do not know of the plight of the king."

"We cannot wait for the Goths. The king will either be dead or long gone when they eventually arrive", I replied.

We were not the kind of men who were content to sit and wait. "Let us gather the fit warriors and ride to the fort. Mayhap Arash will provide a solution."

Gordas, Elmanos and I rode at the head of the twelve hundred warriors. It would have been arrogant to call it an army. It was a warband.

We encountered Roman auxiliary scouts who simply retreated at our advance.

Cresting the familiar hill, we overlooked the battleground of the day before. Our dead had been left where they had fallen.

In front of the hillfort a mounted army was arrayed for battle. On the right flank were the Carpiani warriors, at least three thousand. On the left, a thousand Roman auxiliaries. Of the huge army we clashed with the previous day, there was no sign.

"Let us go hear what the snake has to say", I said, reining in half a mile from the enemy.

Gordas spat with contempt. "I will put my lasso around his neck and drag him behind my horse until he has been flayed alive."

I sighed, for once sharing the Hun's view. "Let us first see what he has to say. Remember, he holds the king."

We advanced with our arms extended to the side, palms facing upwards. Halfway between the armies we came to a halt. I noticed a contingent separate from the Roman auxiliaries, riding towards the Carpiani. There we could see them exchange words until, reluctantly, seven men trotted their horses in our direction. It was a breach of the customs of parley, as we were outnumbered.

Gordas growled like the savage beast he was. "Tarbus will try to kill us. See, he is accompanied by Romans only."

"He might", I conceded.

"If he does, leave the snake to me", was his only retort.

More than three hundred paces separated us from both armies, too far for a Carpiani arrow to find its mark.

Gordas sat on his horse, grinning. Elmanos wore much the same expression. "What have you been up to?" I asked.

The Urugundi was the one to answer. "Yes, we have talked", he said, affirming my suspicion.

Elmanos enlightened me. "We have spoken to the warriors. Today is as good a day to die as any, lord. In fact, it is better than most."

I looked at him quizzically.

"We all know that the god speaks to you, lord", Elmanos said. "If we fight bravely and die, we will be allowed into the feast-tent of Arash. The god will welcome you and accept us because we are your companions."

Suddenly I understood the dream. Arash wished for me to fight, even against overwhelming odds. I felt strangely calm, at peace with my destiny. At least Hostilius, Marcus, Vibius and Cai would be spared. They would return to the Thervingi and care for my family, of that I was sure.

Gordas whispered, reverently. "Our tale will survive, Eochar. Our names will be spoken around the cooking fires on the Sea of Grass for generations to come."

The individuals in the enemy parley group became recognizable as they approached. I immediately noticed Tarbus, magnificently fitted out in his gilded scale armour.

My eyes left the Carpiani king to study the Romans. The tribune leading them was none other than Adherbal the Numidian.

Tarbus came to a halt. A distance less than the length of a horse separated us. The rest of his party flanked him, but they were at least three paces behind.

The Carpiani king smiled the way I imagined a viper would at an unfortunate rat.

"It seems that we are fighting on opposite sides, prince Eochar. I have negotiated a peace on behalf of the Carpiani and the Goths. The emperor was here in person." He triumphantly held up a scroll.

Anger welled up inside me at the mention of the name of Philip the Arab, but I displayed a face of stone.

"Where is the king?" I asked.

The moment I spoke, I noticed recognition dawn in the eyes of the Numidian tribune. A smile touched his lips for an instant but he said naught.

"I expected that you would have worked it out for yourself by now", he mocked. "But allow me to enlighten you. The emperor requires a victory to cement his position and silence his critics. I have given him that, as well as proof in that regard. Bradakos is the proof that he will take to Rome." He waved his arm to the side. "And these Roxolani corpses are the price of that victory."

"The Goths will rip you apart, traitor", Gordas growled.

Tarbus answered me instead. "Keep your Hun dog on a leash."

He smiled. "But I will answer anyway, as I am a benevolent king."

"The Goths will do no such thing. All they know is that we were surrounded and that the Roxolani failed to drive away the Romans. I was forced to make peace, yes, but I secured a payment in gold. A fortune. This gold I will pass on to the Goths, in full."

I grasped at a straw. "Tarbus, we are both from the royal line of the Scythians. According to custom I now challenge you to combat, with the crown of the Carpiani as the prize."

The Carpiani king doubled over, laughing out loud. "You must surely think me a fool. I reject your challenge on the grounds that I cannot fight a dead man. Why do you think I tell you all these things without a care? You will bleed your lifeblood away into this dust today, Roman mongrel."

He lifted his hand and the call of a buccina echoed across the plain.

From behind the crests of the hills overlooking our position, thousands upon thousands of horsemen appeared.

Tarbus again gestured towards the warriors surrounding us. "Behold your demise", he sneered. "You were so worried about the king, you rode into the trap like a child would. You are nothing but an idiot, god-messenger."

I breathed deeply, ready to meet my destiny. Tribune Adherbal's eyes kept flicking to the hills nervously, which confused me.

"They are not our men", the Numidian hissed in Latin.

Tarbus turned white as a newly bleached tunic and looked from side to side at the horde descending the distant hills.

The Carpiani pointed his finger at me and snarled. "Kill him, Moor."

No one moved. "Do it yourself, barbarian", Adherbal said, inclining his head to me. "Greetings, tribune Domitius."

I acknowledged his words with a smile and a slight nod.

Around us the horde of Goths came to a halt, and a group of men on horseback advanced in our direction. I soon recognized the grinning face of Kniva, with a martial-looking Ostrogotha riding at his side. Hostilius was half-dragging a man behind him, the prisoner's hands tied to the end of a lasso.

He motioned with his head towards Decaeneus, the enaree. "Look who I ran into, Domitius. It's 'the one who knows'." Hostilius jerked the rope, causing the shaman to stumble.

"He sang like a newsgiver in the forum. Even before the Goths started working on him", he said, grinning wickedly.

Ostrogotha nudged his horse until he was but two paces away from me.

The high king of the Greuthungi turned his gaze of iron on Tarbus, who visibly recoiled.

"Prince Eochar has challenged me to single combat", Tarbus wailed. "I will accept, if you grant me my freedom when I defeat him."

"Eochar cannot fight a man who is dead already", the Goth king growled. He gestured to his burly guards who dragged Tarbus from his saddle.

The Greuthungi king spoke: "Your man from Serica divined that you would require our assistance and my son Kniva owes you a life. That debt is now paid. We fell upon your ambushers and killed many."

I inclined my head in thanks towards Ostrogotha and Kniva. "I would ask that you grant me a boon, lords."

Ostrogotha raised his eyebrows and gave me a slight nod, allowing me to state my request.

I pointed to Adherbal and his Numidians. "I know this man. He is from the land of the Moors across the Middle Sea. He has honour. I beg that you allow them to leave this place unharmed."

Kniva nodded and Ostrogotha turned to one of his warleaders. "You have heard the words of the prince. Let it be as he says."

I walked my horse alongside the Numidian tribune's mount. "You and your men are free to go, my friend", I said and clasped his arm.

He eyed me with disbelief, but nodded in acceptance. "The one you call Bradakos has been taken to Rome. He is not badly injured. Soon the celebrations of a thousand years will commence. The emperor will parade him through the streets and he will die in the arena. That much I have heard."

I clasped his arm. "Look after the son of Simsek", I said, and slapped the Hun horse on its muscled rump.

Kniva took the rope attached to the shaman from Hostilius. "My father-in-law and I will deal with the Carpiani, Eochar."

The Thervingi iudex turned to the enaree, pulling on the rope. "Come Decaeneus, you have to tell your tale once more. Be helpful and your death will be quick. Lie, and I will give you to the Urugundi. Did you know that unlike the Goths, they do not have a word in their tongue for 'mercy'?"

"Tonight, Eochar, we will sup together and talk about the future", he said, and rode away.

* * *

I later heard that the enaree had told all.

Enraged by their treachery, the Carpiani nobles demanded that Tarbus and Decaeneus be handed over to them.

Ostrogotha conceded, but to honour his oath, he opened the shaman's throat before he fell into the hands of his own people.

303

Tarbus, on the other hand, was not as fortunate.

Chapter 38 – Cleansing

I returned to my tent with a heavy heart. Bradakos, my friend and mentor, was on his way to Rome in chains. He would be kept alive for many moons before Philip the Arab displays him as a trophy of war. Ultimately his life would end to entertain the masses in Rome. An unfitting demise for a man such as the king of the Roxolani.

I was permeated with dust and sweat so I walked to a nearby meltwater stream to rid myself of the grime.

Back at my tent I stripped my armour and meticulously cleaned and polished every hoof scale.

I rubbed all the leather parts using the oil that the Scythians rendered from the shinbones of cattle. Then I spent forever putting a shine on my helmet, meticulously polishing it with the fine wood ash left in the firepit.

None came to visit, as I had demanded to be left alone.

When I was done, I dressed in my best tunic and donned my full armour.

I closed the flap of the tent and placed hemp seeds on the red-hot stones. I sat down in the middle of the tent cross-legged, and breathed the way that Cai had taught me.

Then I prayed to the god of war and fire.

I mounted the dreamhorse and ascended to the abode of the gods.

The fog in my mind slowly dissipated, and my path became clear as daylight.

I was brought back to the present by a familiar voice. "Domitius, are you still on this side of the river?"

I opened the flap and stepped outside, the cold evening air reviving me.

I smiled, suddenly hungry, my vigour restored. "Let us go and enjoy the hospitality of the kings, Primus Pilus", I said.

Hostilius eyed me suspiciously.

"Gordas tells me that you were ready to die in battle this morning. Then you skulk off, looking like you are going to open your veins or fall on your bloody sword. You hide in the tent all afternoon inhaling the shaman smoke and we hear you scream like a stuck pig." He shook his head from side to side, emphasizing his point.

"Then you walk from the tent two watches later, all polished up like the god of war himself. And suddenly you're chirpy and all smiles."

"It is because tonight, Primus Pilus, the war god has gifted me something I did not possess this morning", I said.

"Show me", he said.

"That I cannot do", I replied.

A frown crossed his brow.

I slapped him on the shoulder.

"But I can tell you", I grinned, and I shared Arash's plan.

Historical Note

I do not elaborate where I believe that it might be a spoiler for future books.

Characters

Eochar - Lucius Domitius Aurelianus, or Aurelian as he is better known, I believe, was the most accomplished Roman to ever walk this earth. Some would disagree, which is their right. Little is known about his whereabouts during the period covered by this book.

In time, all will be revealed, but for now I will leave you with a few quotes from the surviving records.

From the English Translation of the (much-disputed) *Historia Augusta Volume III*:

"Aurelian, born of humble parents and from his earliest years very quick of mind and famous for his strength, never let a day go by, even though a feast-day or a day of leisure, on which he did not practise with the spear, the bow and arrow, and other exercises in arms."

"... he was a comely man, good to look upon because of his manly grace, rather tall in stature, and very strong in his muscles; he was a little too fond of wine and food, but he indulged his passions rarely; he exercised the greatest severity and a discipline that had no equal, being extremely ready to draw his sword."

"..."Aurelian Sword-in-hand," and so he would be identified."

"... in the war against the Sarmatians Aurelian with his own hand slew forty-eight men in a single day and that in the course of several days he slew over nine hundred and fifty, so that the boys even composed in his honour the following jingles and dance-ditties, to which they would dance on holidays in soldier fashion:

"Thousand, thousand, thousand we've beheaded now.

One alone, a thousand we've beheaded now.

He shall drink a thousand who a thousand slew.

So much wine is owned by no one as the blood which he has shed."

Marcus - Marcus Aurelius Claudius was an actual person, famous in history, and I believe a close friend of Lucius Domitius.

Cai is a figment of my imagination. The Roman Empire had contact with China, or Serica, as it was called then. His origins, training methods and fighting style I have researched in detail. Cai, to me, represents the seldom written about influence of China on the Roman Empire.

Primus Pilus Hostilius Proculus is a fictional character. He represents the core of the legions. The hardened plebeian officer.

Gordas – The fictional Hun/Urugundi general. Otto J Maenschen-Helfen writes in his book, The World of the Huns, that he believed the Urugundi to be a Hunnic tribe. Zosimus, the ancient Byzantine writer, mentions the Urugundi in an alliance with the Goths and the Scythians during the mid-third century AD. (Maenchen-Helfen's book is fascinating. He could read Russian, Persian, Greek and Chinese, enabling him to interpret the original primary texts.)

Vibius Marcellinus was an actual person. He will feature more later.

Segelinde – the Gothic princess, is an invention. However, Ulpia Severina, the woman who was married to Aurelian, is not.

Lucius's Contubernia – Ursa, Silentus, Pumilio and Felix. They were not actual people, but represent the common soldiers within the Roman Legions.

310

Bradakos – King Bradakos of the Roxolani never lived.

Ostrogotha the Patient – king of the Greuthungi. He was the son of Hisarna (the Iron One) the son of Amal (the Fortunate One), from there the Amaling Dynasty of the Goths. The reason why he was called 'The Patient', I have concocted.

Kniva was the king of the Goths during the mid-third century AD. He was not the brother-in-law of Aurelian, but he is famous for his deeds. All will be revealed.

Tarbus – King of the Carpiani. The Carpiani must have had a king, who he was, I do not know.

Transsilvanian storyline

Herodotus wrote about the Venedi and the Fenni in 450 BC. I took the liberty to assume that these peoples were related to the later Slavs as described in Maurice's Strategikon, which was written in the sixth century AD.

Philip the Arab ceased the payment of the subsidies to the tribes north of the Danube shortly after coming into power.

Resultantly the Carpiani/Scythians/Goths did invade Dacia and Moesia in 245 AD. They moved through Dacia, plundered Transsilvania, then crossed the Danube into Moesia.

Shortly after, the Limes Transalutanus was abandoned by Rome for many years.

The emperor at the time, Philip the Arab, sent Senator Decius to repel the Scythian invasion.

Decius was less than content with the performance of the legions, culminating in his dismissal of many legionaries, who ended up joining Ostrogotha.

Phillip did pursue the Scythians across the border of Dacia into the tribal lands, utilising African Berber cavalry. He trapped the Carpiani in a fortress, but eventually concluded a peace on lenient terms and rushed back to Rome. In all likeliness, he was fleeing from the allies of the Carpiani who had come to relieve the siege.

Were Philip the Arab and his brother Priscus really the bad guys? I quote from the English translation of the works of Zosimus:

"... Priscus, their governor, who was a man of an intolerably evil disposition... "

Make up your own mind.

Random items

The Chinese powdered Chrysanthemum flowers for the use as an insecticide as early as 1000 BC. Even today, Pyrethrin, the active ingredient, is still used to kill lice.

Scythicon was an evil poison brewed by the Scythians. The details in the book are near accurate.

"The one who tries", is an ancient runic inscription found on a spear-blade.

The Paduroaia and the Strigoi are local legends of Transylvania. The same applies to the fog being a little girl.

The names of the woods like Mad Forest, Screaming Woods and Heinous Forest are real. The barrier created by the haunted, near impenetrable woods of old, is one theory explaining the lack of an outer ditch on a portion of the Limes Transalutanus, north of Izbasesti.

The Scythian enarees are real.

The route I have described through Transylvania (Roman Transsilvania) is geographically accurate. I did use modern place names where I was unable to determine the ancient name. The route taken by the invaders in 245 AD is not known, although the fort at Rucar was destroyed by fire during this time.

Author's Note

I trust that you have enjoyed the fourth book in the series.

In many instances, written history relating to this period has either been lost in the fog of time, or it might never have been recorded. That is especially applicable to most of the tribes which Rome referred to as barbarians. These peoples did not record history by writing it down. They only appear in the written histories of the Greeks, Romans, Persians and Chinese, who often regarded them as enemies.

In any event, my aim is to be as historically accurate as possible, but I am sure that I inadvertently miss the target from time to time, in which case I apologise to the purists among my readers.

Kindly take the time to provide a rating and/or a review.

I will keep you updated via my blog with regards to the progress on the fifth book in the series.

Feel free to contact me any time via my website. I will respond.

www.HectorMillerBooks.com

Made in the USA
Columbia, SC
07 January 2020